SON OF SUPERMAN

HOWARD CHAYKIN
DAVID TISCHMAN

writers

J.H. WILLIAMS III

penciller

MICK GRAY

inker

LEE LOUGHRIDGE

colorist

KURT HATHAWAY

letterer

Superman created by
JERRY SIEGEL &
JOE SHUSTER

TM

JENETTE KAHN
president & editor-in-chief

PAUL LEVITZ
executive vice president & publisher

MIKE CARLIN
executive editor

ANDY HELFER
group editor

JIM HIGGINS
assistant editor

GEORG BREWER
design director

AMIE BROCKWAY
art director

RICHARD BRUNING
vp-creative director

PATRICK CALDON
vp-finance & operations

DOROTHY CROUCH
vp-licensed publishing

TERRI CUNNINGHAM
vp-managing editor

JOEL EHRLICH
senior vp-advertising & promotions

ALISON GILL
executive director-manufacturing

LILLIAN LASERSON
vp & general counsel

JIM LEE
editorial director- wildstorm

JOHN NEE
vp & general manager-wildstorm

BOB WAYNE
vp-direct sales

SON OF SUPERMAN.
Published by DC Comics,
1700 Broadway,
New York, NY 10019.
Copyright © 1999 DC Comics.
All Rights Reserved.
All characters featured in this issue,
the distinctive likenesses thereof,
and all related indicia are trademarks
of DC Comics. The stories, characters
and incidents mentioned in this
magazine are entirely fictional.
Printed on recyclable paper.
DC Comics. A division of Warner Bros.-
A Time Warner Entertainment Company.

Printed in Canada. First printing.

Hard Cover ISBN: 1-56389-595-1
Soft Cover ISBN: 1-56389-596-X

Publication design by Kim Grzybek.

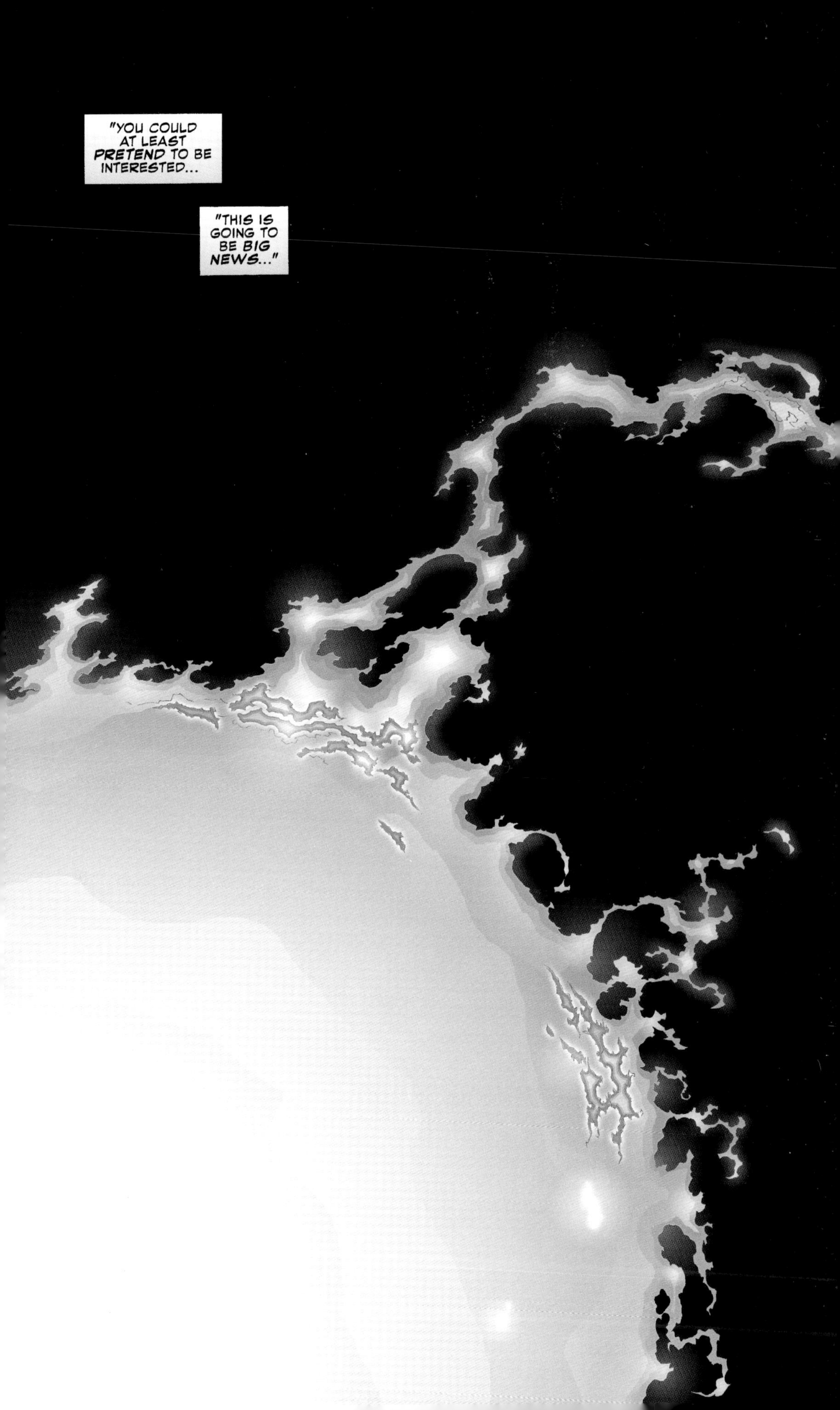
"YOU COULD AT LEAST PRETEND TO BE INTERESTED...
"THIS IS GOING TO BE BIG NEWS..."

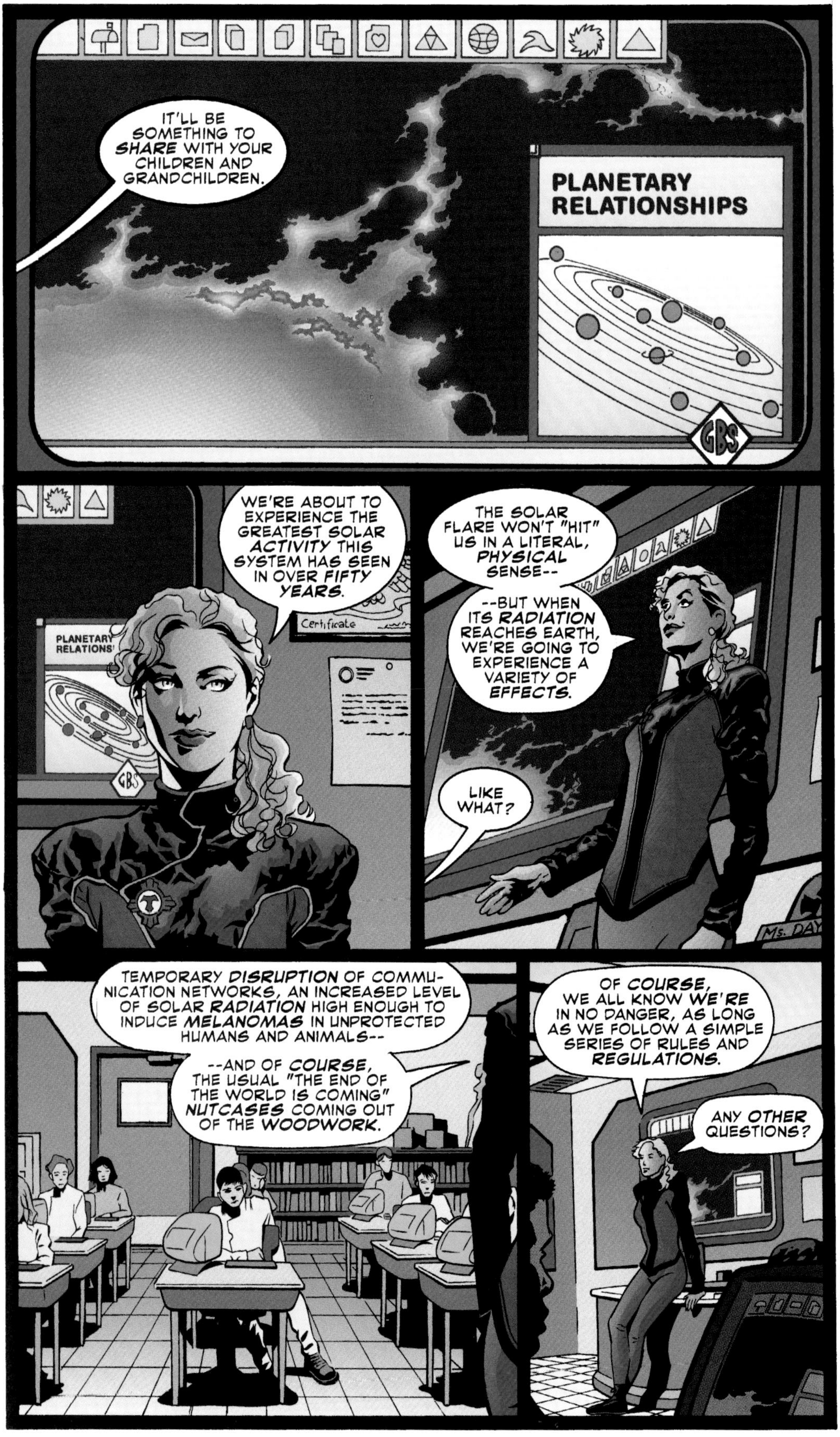
IT'LL BE SOMETHING TO SHARE WITH YOUR CHILDREN AND GRANDCHILDREN.
PLANETARY RELATIONSHIPS
GBS
WE'RE ABOUT TO EXPERIENCE THE GREATEST SOLAR ACTIVITY THIS SYSTEM HAS SEEN IN OVER FIFTY YEARS.
PLANETARY RELATIONS
Certificate
GBS
THE SOLAR FLARE WON'T "HIT" US IN A LITERAL, PHYSICAL SENSE--
--BUT WHEN ITS RADIATION REACHES EARTH, WE'RE GOING TO EXPERIENCE A VARIETY OF EFFECTS.
LIKE WHAT?
Ms. DAY
TEMPORARY DISRUPTION OF COMMUNICATION NETWORKS, AN INCREASED LEVEL OF SOLAR RADIATION HIGH ENOUGH TO INDUCE MELANOMAS IN UNPROTECTED HUMANS AND ANIMALS--
--AND OF COURSE, THE USUAL "THE END OF THE WORLD IS COMING" NUTCASES COMING OUT OF THE WOODWORK.
OF COURSE, WE ALL KNOW WE'RE IN NO DANGER, AS LONG AS WE FOLLOW A SIMPLE SERIES OF RULES AND REGULATIONS.
ANY OTHER QUESTIONS?

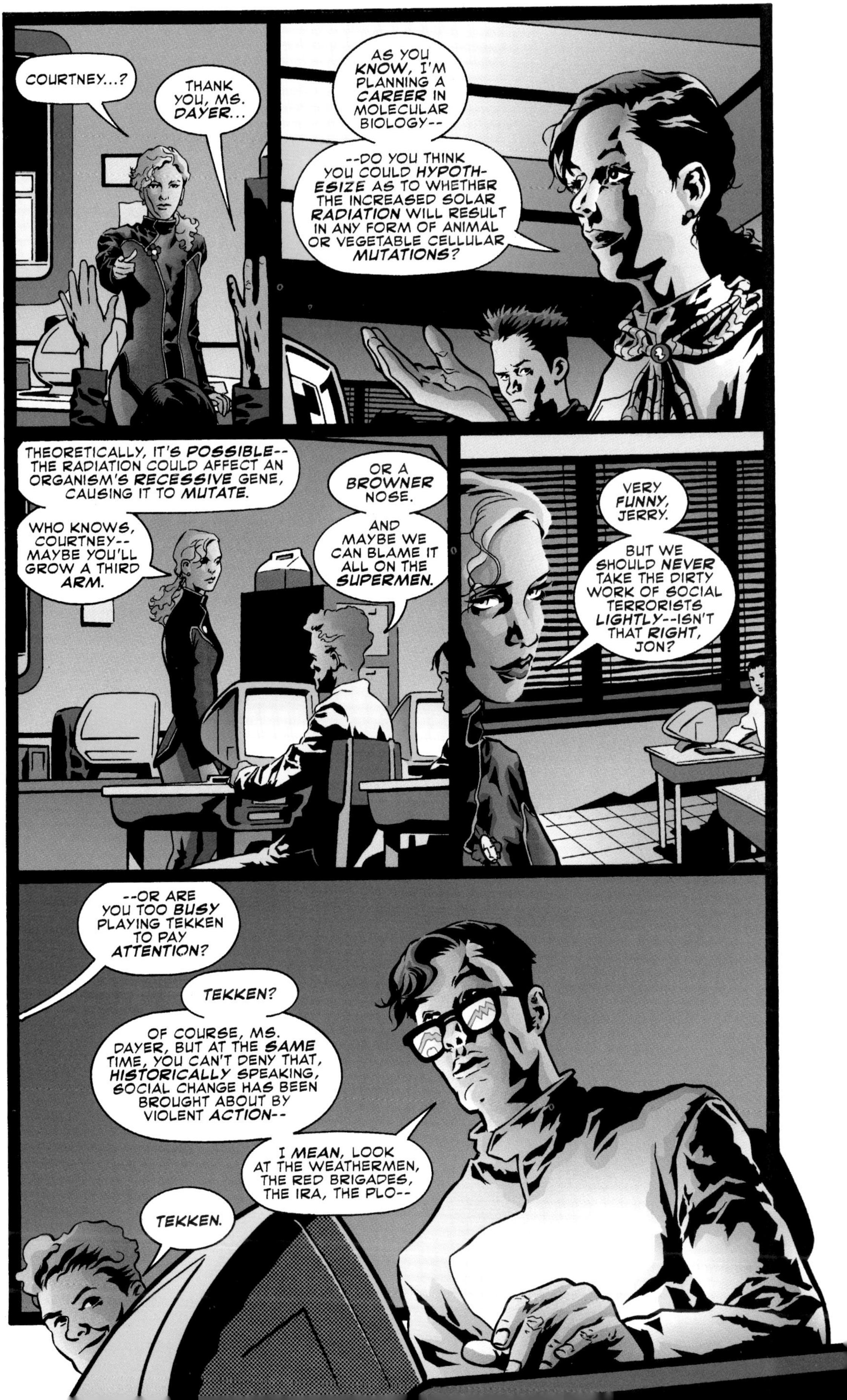
COURTNEY...?
THANK YOU, MS. DAYER...
AS YOU KNOW, I'M PLANNING A CAREER IN MOLECULAR BIOLOGY--
--DO YOU THINK YOU COULD HYPOTHESIZE AS TO WHETHER THE INCREASED SOLAR RADIATION WILL RESULT IN ANY FORM OF ANIMAL OR VEGETABLE CELLULAR MUTATIONS?
THEORETICALLY, IT'S POSSIBLE-- THE RADIATION COULD AFFECT AN ORGANISM'S RECESSIVE GENE, CAUSING IT TO MUTATE.
WHO KNOWS, COURTNEY-- MAYBE YOU'LL GROW A THIRD ARM.
OR A BROWNER NOSE.
AND MAYBE WE CAN BLAME IT ALL ON THE SUPERMEN.
VERY FUNNY, JERRY.
BUT WE SHOULD NEVER TAKE THE DIRTY WORK OF SOCIAL TERRORISTS LIGHTLY--ISN'T THAT RIGHT, JON?
--OR ARE YOU TOO BUSY PLAYING TEKKEN TO PAY ATTENTION?
TEKKEN?
OF COURSE, MS. DAYER, BUT AT THE SAME TIME, YOU CAN'T DENY THAT, HISTORICALLY SPEAKING, SOCIAL CHANGE HAS BEEN BROUGHT ABOUT BY VIOLENT ACTION--
I MEAN, LOOK AT THE WEATHERMEN, THE RED BRIGADES, THE IRA, THE PLO--
TEKKEN.

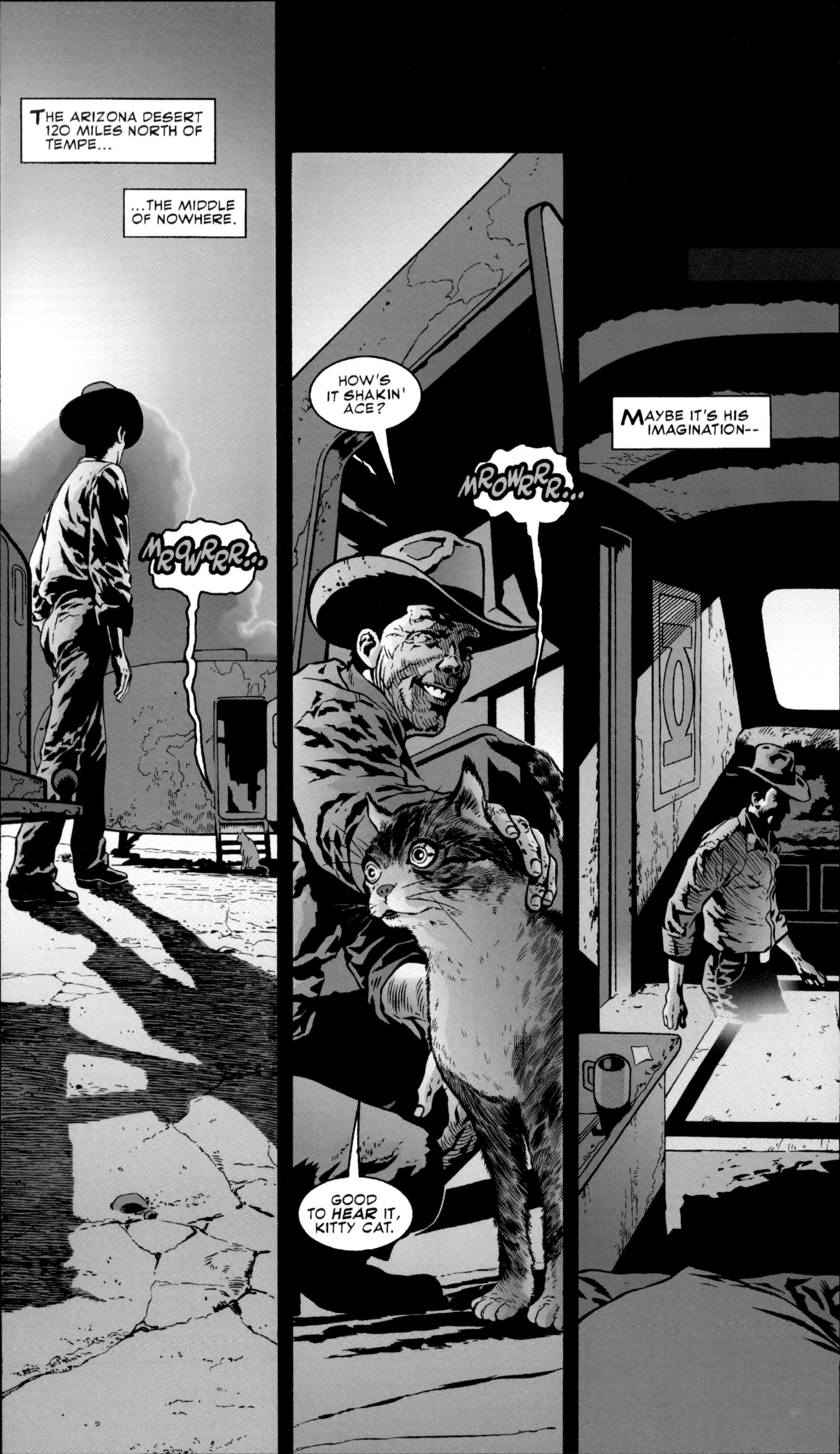
THE ARIZONA DESERT 120 MILES NORTH OF TEMPE...
...THE MIDDLE OF NOWHERE.
MROWRRR...
HOW'S IT SHAKIN' ACE?
MROWRRR...
GOOD TO HEAR IT, KITTY CAT.
MAYBE IT'S HIS IMAGINATION--

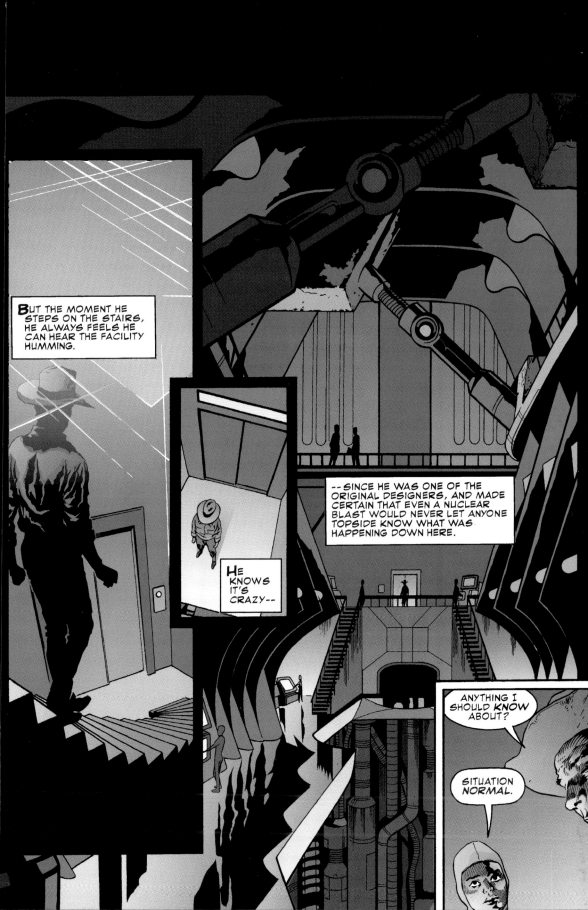

BUT THE MOMENT HE STEPS ON THE STAIRS, HE ALWAYS FEELS HE CAN HEAR THE FACILITY HUMMING.

HE KNOWS IT'S CRAZY--

-- SINCE HE WAS ONE OF THE ORIGINAL DESIGNERS, AND MADE CERTAIN THAT EVEN A NUCLEAR BLAST WOULD NEVER LET ANYONE TOPSIDE KNOW WHAT WAS HAPPENING DOWN HERE.

ANYTHING I SHOULD KNOW ABOUT?

SITUATION NORMAL.

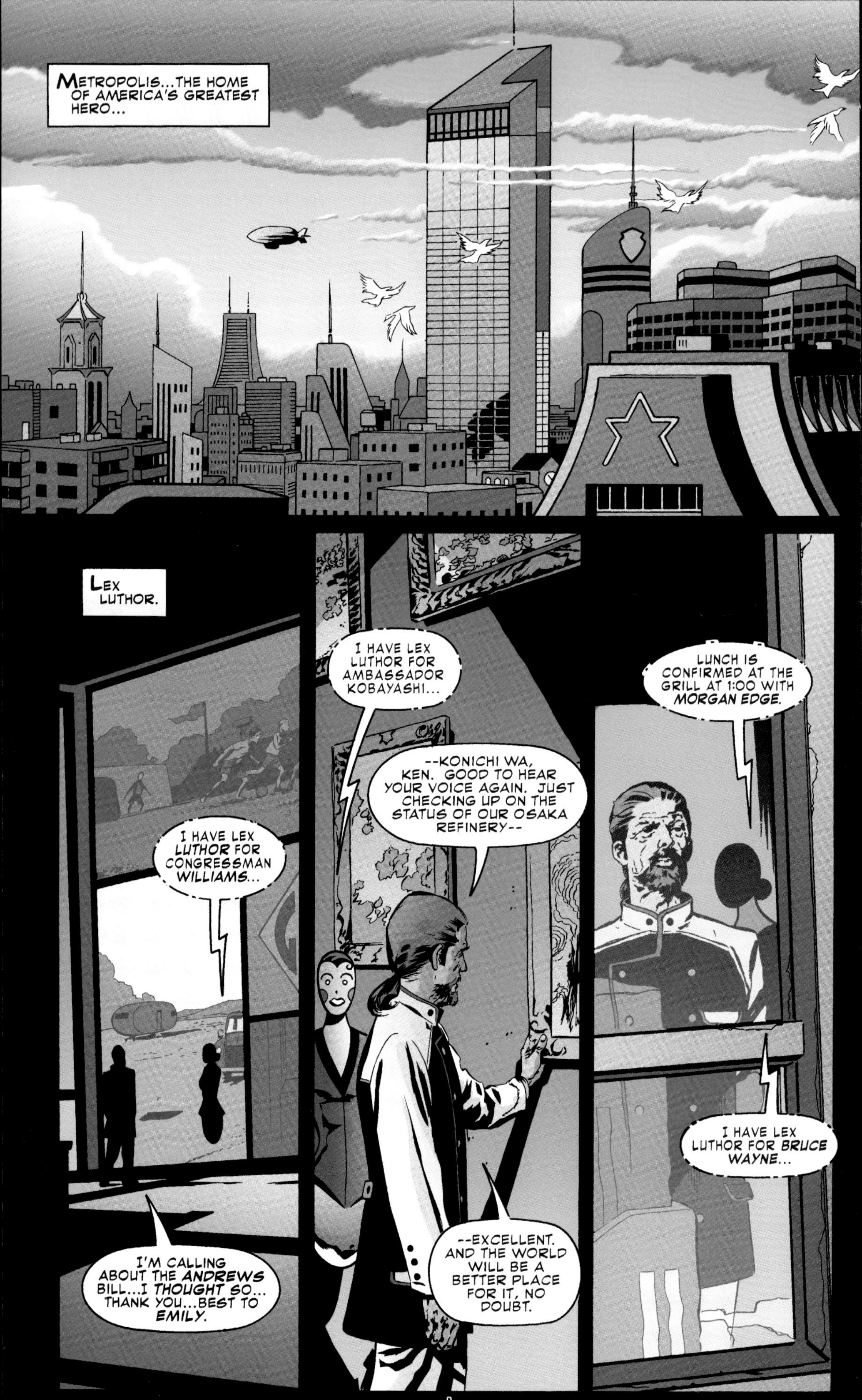
METROPOLIS...THE HOME OF AMERICA'S GREATEST HERO...
LEX LUTHOR.
I HAVE LEX LUTHOR FOR CONGRESSMAN WILLIAMS...
I'M CALLING ABOUT THE ANDREWS BILL...I THOUGHT SO... THANK YOU...BEST TO EMILY.
I HAVE LEX LUTHOR FOR AMBASSADOR KOBAYASHI...
--KONICHI WA, KEN. GOOD TO HEAR YOUR VOICE AGAIN. JUST CHECKING UP ON THE STATUS OF OUR OSAKA REFINERY--
--EXCELLENT. AND THE WORLD WILL BE A BETTER PLACE FOR IT, NO DOUBT.
LUNCH IS CONFIRMED AT THE GRILL AT 1:00 WITH MORGAN EDGE.
I HAVE LEX LUTHOR FOR BRUCE WAYNE...

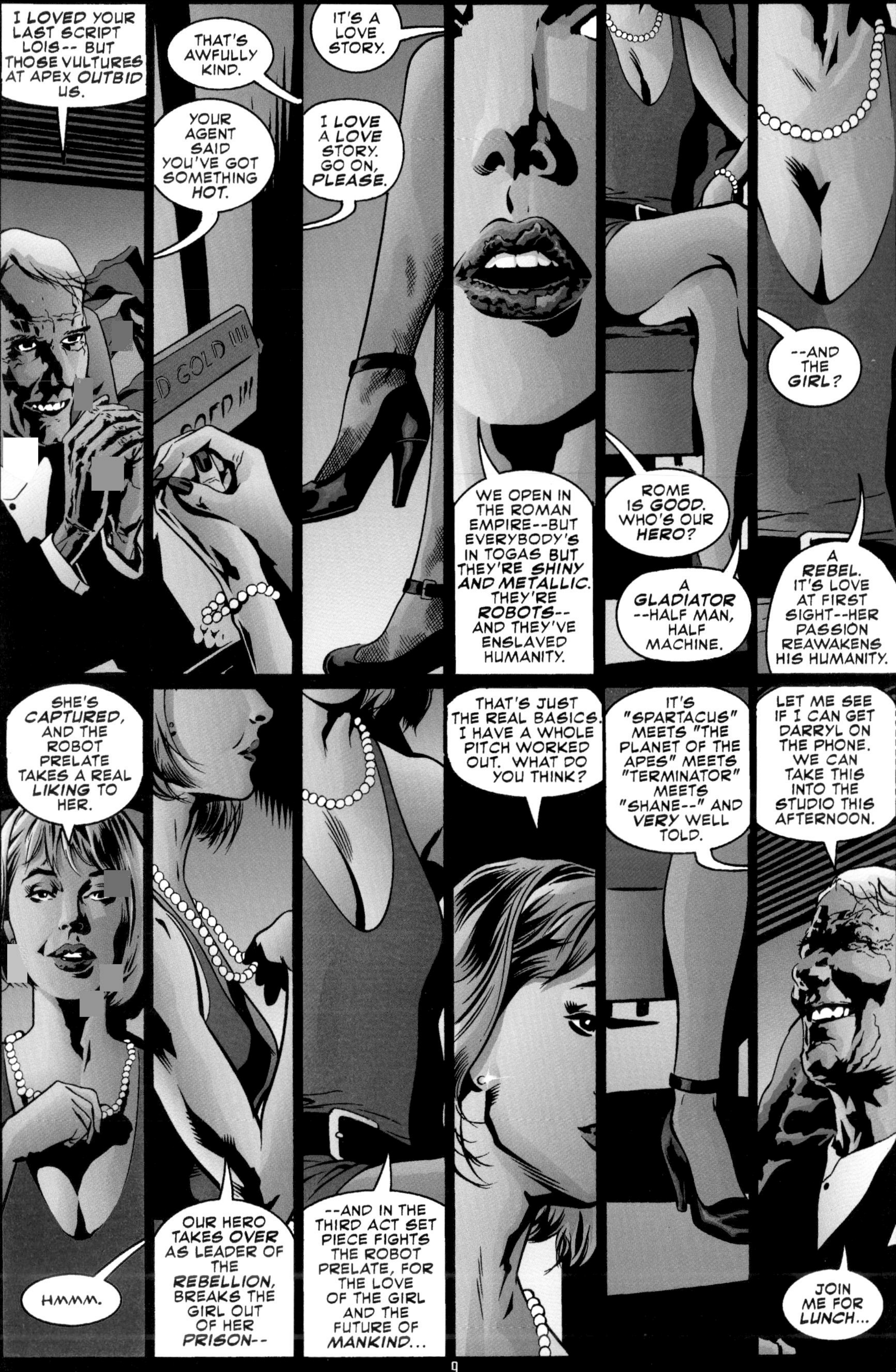

I LOVED YOUR LAST SCRIPT LOIS-- BUT THOSE VULTURES AT APEX OUTBID US.
THAT'S AWFULLY KIND.
YOUR AGENT SAID YOU'VE GOT SOMETHING HOT.
IT'S A LOVE STORY.
I LOVE A LOVE STORY. GO ON, PLEASE.
WE OPEN IN THE ROMAN EMPIRE--BUT EVERYBODY'S IN TOGAS BUT THEY'RE SHINY AND METALLIC. THEY'RE ROBOTS-- AND THEY'VE ENSLAVED HUMANITY.
ROME IS GOOD. WHO'S OUR HERO?
A GLADIATOR --HALF MAN, HALF MACHINE.
--AND THE GIRL?
A REBEL. IT'S LOVE AT FIRST SIGHT--HER PASSION REAWAKENS HIS HUMANITY.
SHE'S CAPTURED, AND THE ROBOT PRELATE TAKES A REAL LIKING TO HER.
HMMM.
OUR HERO TAKES OVER AS LEADER OF THE REBELLION, BREAKS THE GIRL OUT OF HER PRISON--
--AND IN THE THIRD ACT SET PIECE FIGHTS THE ROBOT PRELATE, FOR THE LOVE OF THE GIRL AND THE FUTURE OF MANKIND...
THAT'S JUST THE REAL BASICS. I HAVE A WHOLE PITCH WORKED OUT. WHAT DO YOU THINK?
IT'S "SPARTACUS" MEETS "THE PLANET OF THE APES" MEETS "TERMINATOR" MEETS "SHANE--" AND VERY WELL TOLD.
LET ME SEE IF I CAN GET DARRYL ON THE PHONE. WE CAN TAKE THIS INTO THE STUDIO THIS AFTERNOON.
JOIN ME FOR LUNCH...

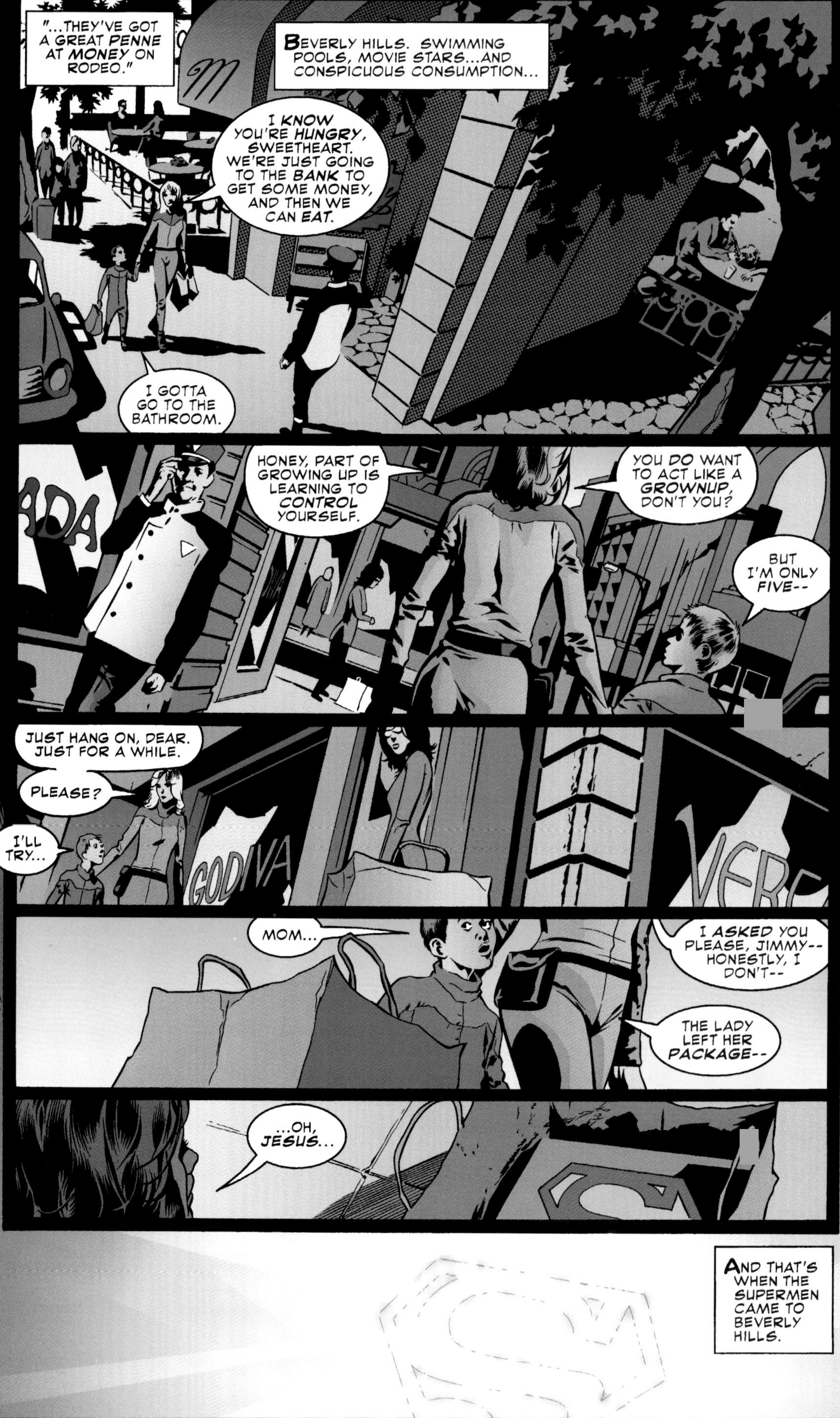
"...THEY'VE GOT A GREAT PENNE AT MONEY ON RODEO."
BEVERLY HILLS. SWIMMING POOLS, MOVIE STARS...AND CONSPICUOUS CONSUMPTION...
I KNOW YOU'RE HUNGRY, SWEETHEART. WE'RE JUST GOING TO THE BANK TO GET SOME MONEY, AND THEN WE CAN EAT.
I GOTTA GO TO THE BATHROOM.
HONEY, PART OF GROWING UP IS LEARNING TO CONTROL YOURSELF.
YOU DO WANT TO ACT LIKE A GROWNUP, DON'T YOU?
BUT I'M ONLY FIVE--
JUST HANG ON, DEAR. JUST FOR A WHILE.
PLEASE?
I'LL TRY...
GODIVA
MOM...
I ASKED YOU PLEASE, JIMMY-- HONESTLY, I DON'T--
THE LADY LEFT HER PACKAGE--
...OH, JESUS...
AND THAT'S WHEN THE SUPERMEN CAME TO BEVERLY HILLS.

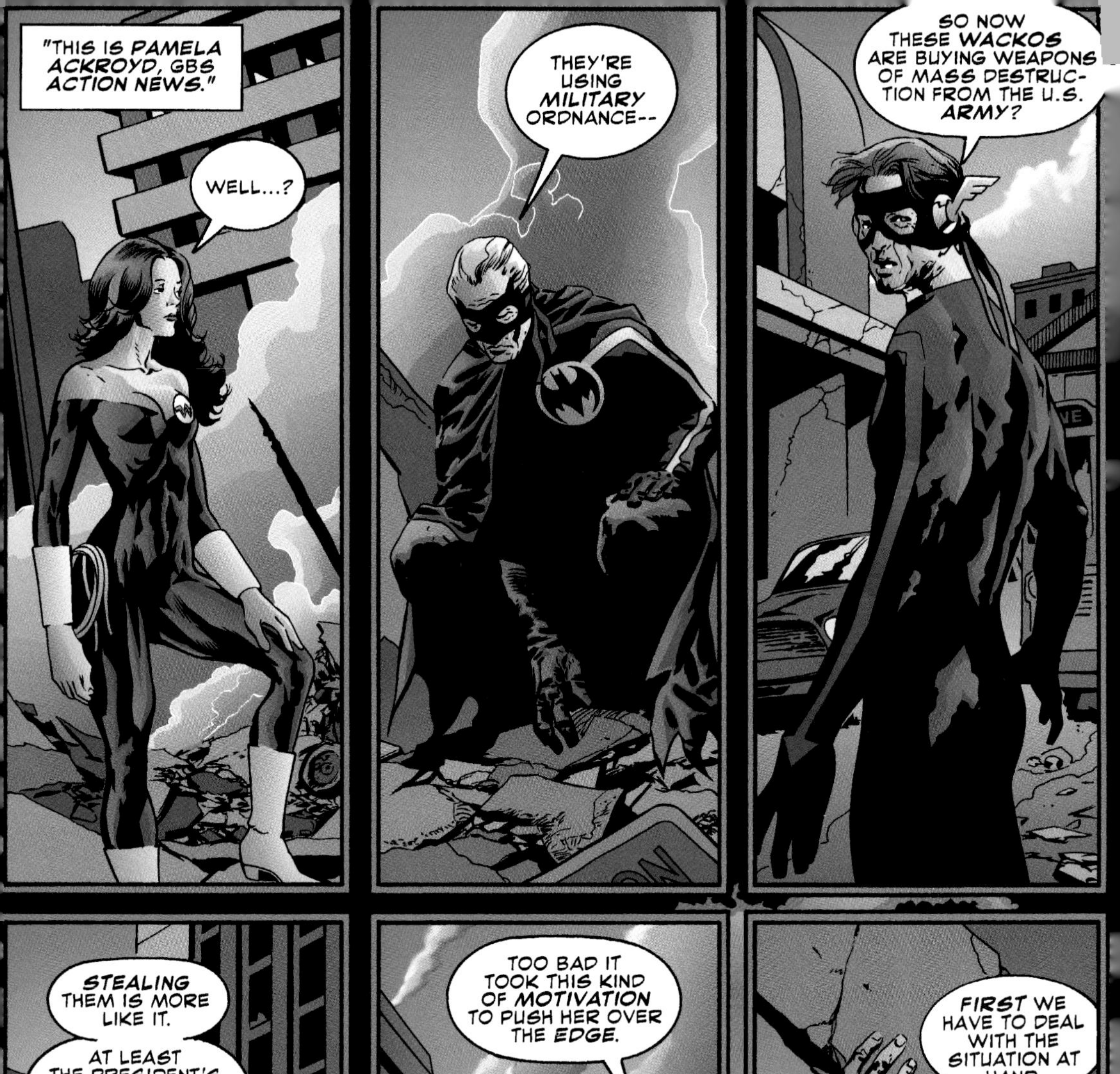
"THIS IS PAMELA ACKROYD, GBS ACTION NEWS."
WELL...?
THEY'RE USING MILITARY ORDNANCE--
SO NOW THESE WACKOS ARE BUYING WEAPONS OF MASS DESTRUCTION FROM THE U.S. ARMY?
STEALING THEM IS MORE LIKE IT.
AT LEAST THE PRESIDENT'S FINALLY GIVEN US THE POWER TO GO AFTER ROSS.
TOO BAD IT TOOK THIS KIND OF MOTIVATION TO PUSH HER OVER THE EDGE.
FIRST WE HAVE TO DEAL WITH THE SITUATION AT HAND.
THESE PEOPLE DON'T JUST VOTE-- THEY'RE CAMPAIGN CONTRIBUTORS.
"IN TODAY'S TOP STORY--"

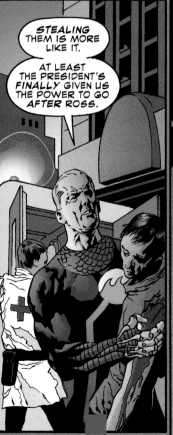

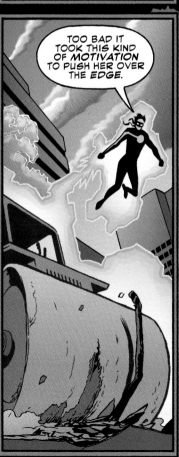

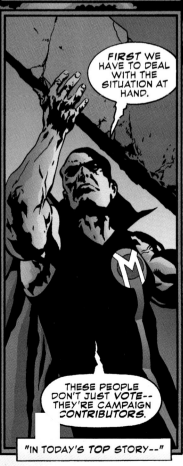

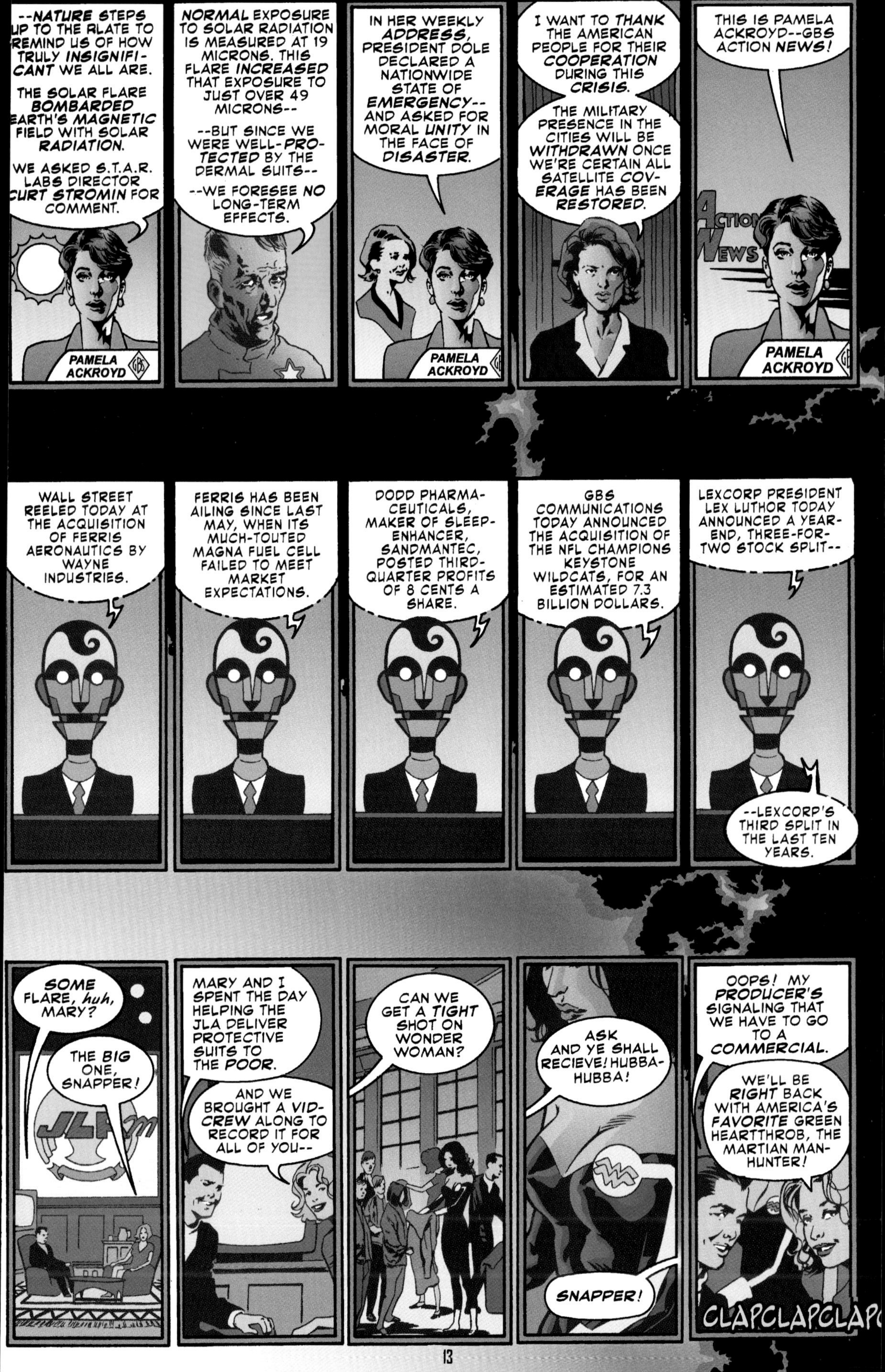
--NATURE STEPS UP TO THE PLATE TO REMIND US OF HOW TRULY INSIGNIFI-CANT WE ALL ARE.
THE SOLAR FLARE BOMBARDED EARTH'S MAGNETIC FIELD WITH SOLAR RADIATION.
WE ASKED S.T.A.R. LABS DIRECTOR CURT STROMIN FOR COMMENT.
PAMELA ACKROYD
GBS
NORMAL EXPOSURE TO SOLAR RADIATION IS MEASURED AT 19 MICRONS. THIS FLARE INCREASED THAT EXPOSURE TO JUST OVER 49 MICRONS--
--BUT SINCE WE WERE WELL-PRO-TECTED BY THE DERMAL SUITS--
--WE FORESEE NO LONG-TERM EFFECTS.
IN HER WEEKLY ADDRESS, PRESIDENT DOLE DECLARED A NATIONWIDE STATE OF EMERGENCY--AND ASKED FOR MORAL UNITY IN THE FACE OF DISASTER.
PAMELA ACKROYD
I WANT TO THANK THE AMERICAN PEOPLE FOR THEIR COOPERATION DURING THIS CRISIS.
THE MILITARY PRESENCE IN THE CITIES WILL BE WITHDRAWN ONCE WE'RE CERTAIN ALL SATELLITE COV-ERAGE HAS BEEN RESTORED.
THIS IS PAMELA ACKROYD--GBS ACTION NEWS!
PAMELA ACKROYD
WALL STREET REELED TODAY AT THE ACQUISITION OF FERRIS AERONAUTICS BY WAYNE INDUSTRIES.
FERRIS HAS BEEN AILING SINCE LAST MAY, WHEN ITS MUCH-TOUTED MAGNA FUEL CELL FAILED TO MEET MARKET EXPECTATIONS.
DODD PHARMA-CEUTICALS, MAKER OF SLEEP-ENHANCER, SANDMANTEC, POSTED THIRD-QUARTER PROFITS OF 8 CENTS A SHARE.
GBS COMMUNICATIONS TODAY ANNOUNCED THE ACQUISITION OF THE NFL CHAMPIONS KEYSTONE WILDCATS, FOR AN ESTIMATED 7.3 BILLION DOLLARS.
LEXCORP PRESIDENT LEX LUTHOR TODAY ANNOUNCED A YEAR-END, THREE-FOR-TWO STOCK SPLIT--
--LEXCORP'S THIRD SPLIT IN THE LAST TEN YEARS.
SOME FLARE, huh, MARY?
THE BIG ONE, SNAPPER!
MARY AND I SPENT THE DAY HELPING THE JLA DELIVER PROTECTIVE SUITS TO THE POOR.
AND WE BROUGHT A VID-CREW ALONG TO RECORD IT FOR ALL OF YOU--
CAN WE GET A TIGHT SHOT ON WONDER WOMAN?
ASK AND YE SHALL RECIEVE! HUBBA-HUBBA!
SNAPPER!
OOPS! MY PRODUCER'S SIGNALING THAT WE HAVE TO GO TO A COMMERCIAL.
WE'LL BE RIGHT BACK WITH AMERICA'S FAVORITE GREEN HEARTTHROB, THE MARTIAN MAN-HUNTER!
CLAPCLAPCLAP

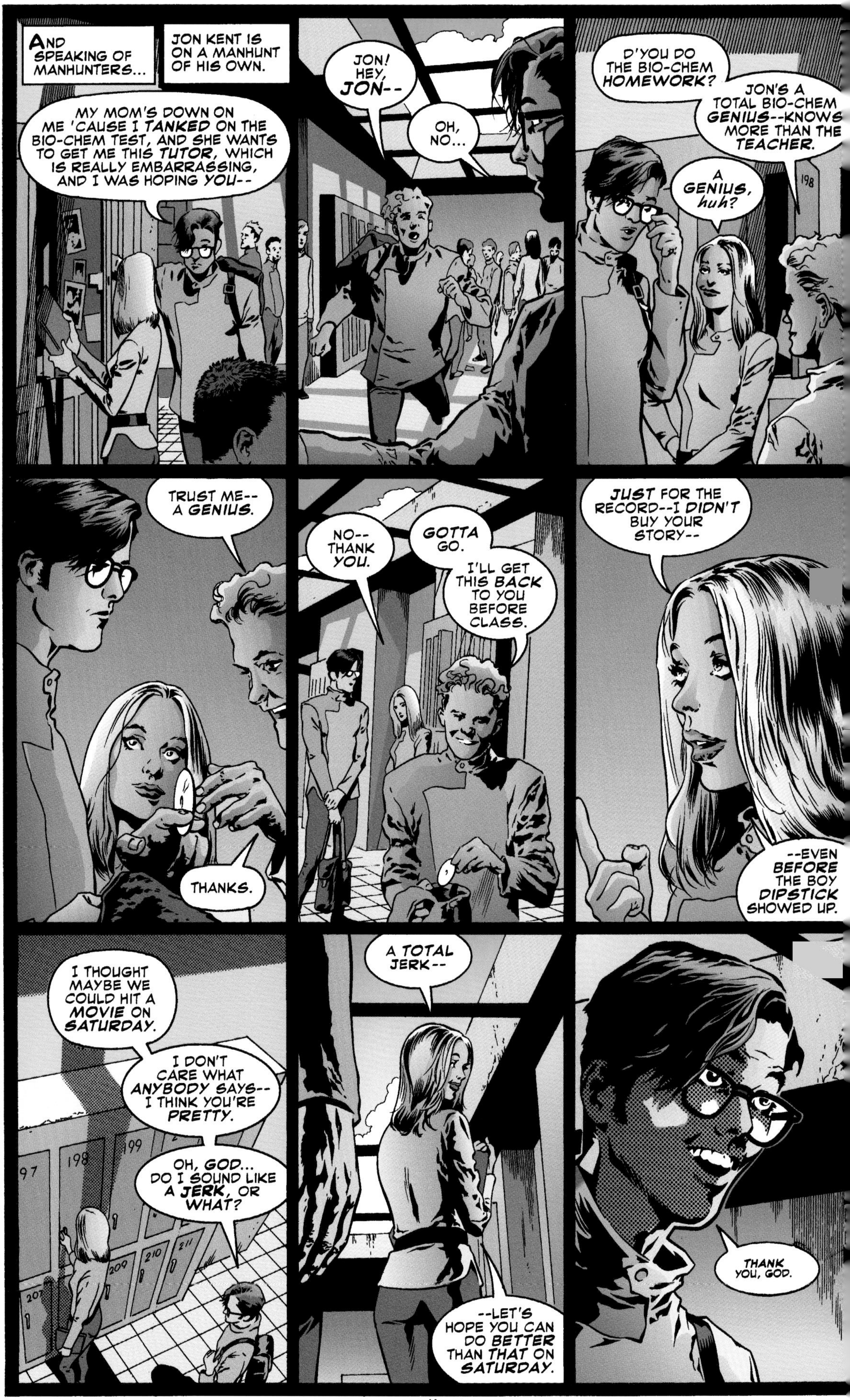

AND SPEAKING OF MANHUNTERS...
JON KENT IS ON A MANHUNT OF HIS OWN.
MY MOM'S DOWN ON ME 'CAUSE I TANKED ON THE BIO-CHEM TEST, AND SHE WANTS TO GET ME THIS TUTOR, WHICH IS REALLY EMBARRASSING, AND I WAS HOPING YOU--
JON! HEY, JON--
OH, NO...
D'YOU DO THE BIO-CHEM HOMEWORK?
JON'S A TOTAL BIO-CHEM GENIUS--KNOWS MORE THAN THE TEACHER.
A GENIUS, huh?
198
TRUST ME-- A GENIUS.
THANKS.
NO-- THANK YOU.
GOTTA GO.
I'LL GET THIS BACK TO YOU BEFORE CLASS.
JUST FOR THE RECORD--I DIDN'T BUY YOUR STORY--
--EVEN BEFORE THE BOY DIPSTICK SHOWED UP.
I THOUGHT MAYBE WE COULD HIT A MOVIE ON SATURDAY.
I DON'T CARE WHAT ANYBODY SAYS-- I THINK YOU'RE PRETTY.
OH, GOD... DO I SOUND LIKE A JERK, OR WHAT?
A TOTAL JERK--
--LET'S HOPE YOU CAN DO BETTER THAN THAT ON SATURDAY.
THANK YOU, GOD.

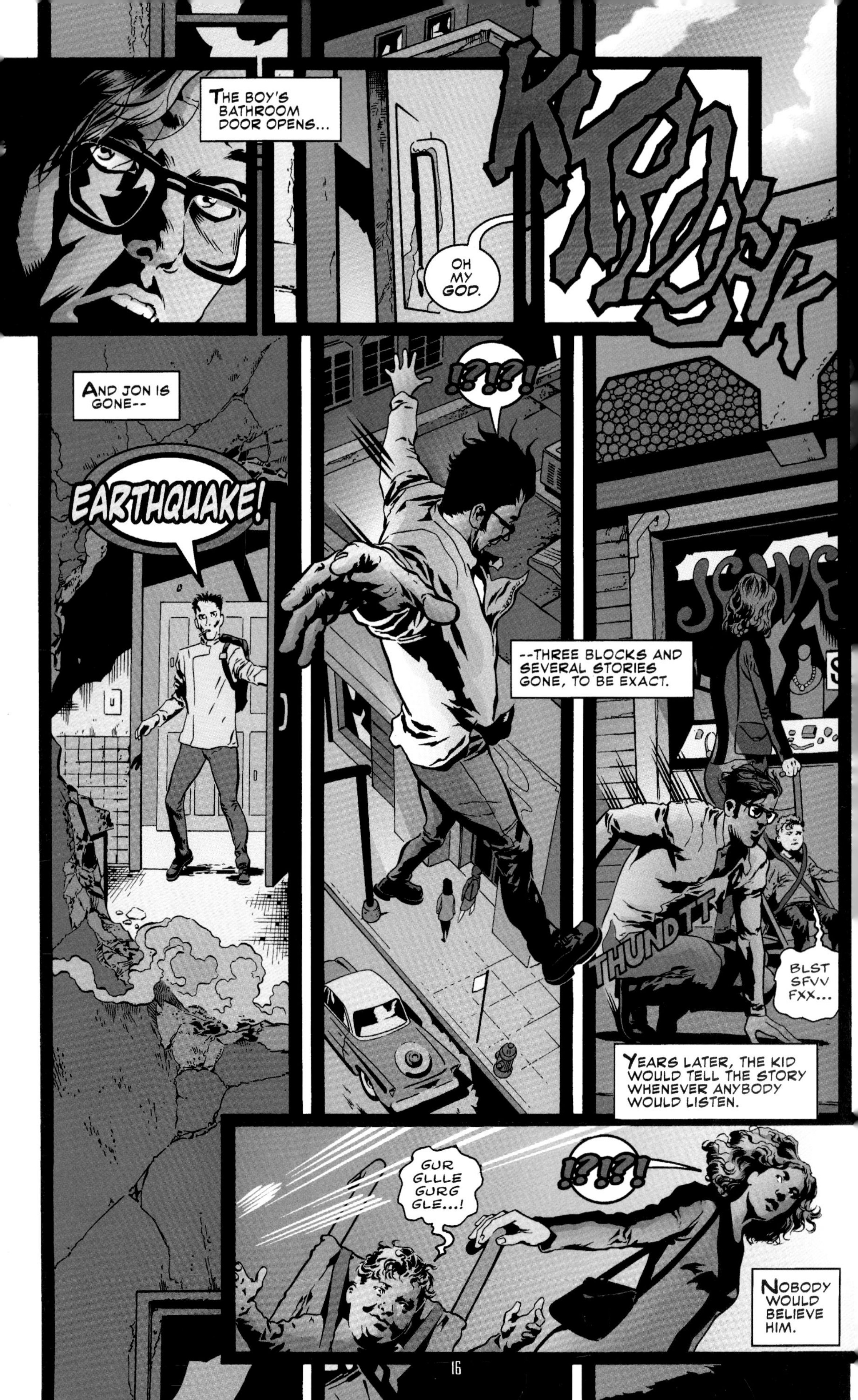
THE BOY'S BATHROOM DOOR OPENS...
OH MY GOD.
KRRTHUNK
AND JON IS GONE--
EARTHQUAKE!
!?!?!
--THREE BLOCKS AND SEVERAL STORIES GONE, TO BE EXACT.
THUNDTT
BLST SFVV FXX...
YEARS LATER, THE KID WOULD TELL THE STORY WHENEVER ANYBODY WOULD LISTEN.
GUR GLLLE GURG GLE...!
!?!?!
NOBODY WOULD BELIEVE HIM.

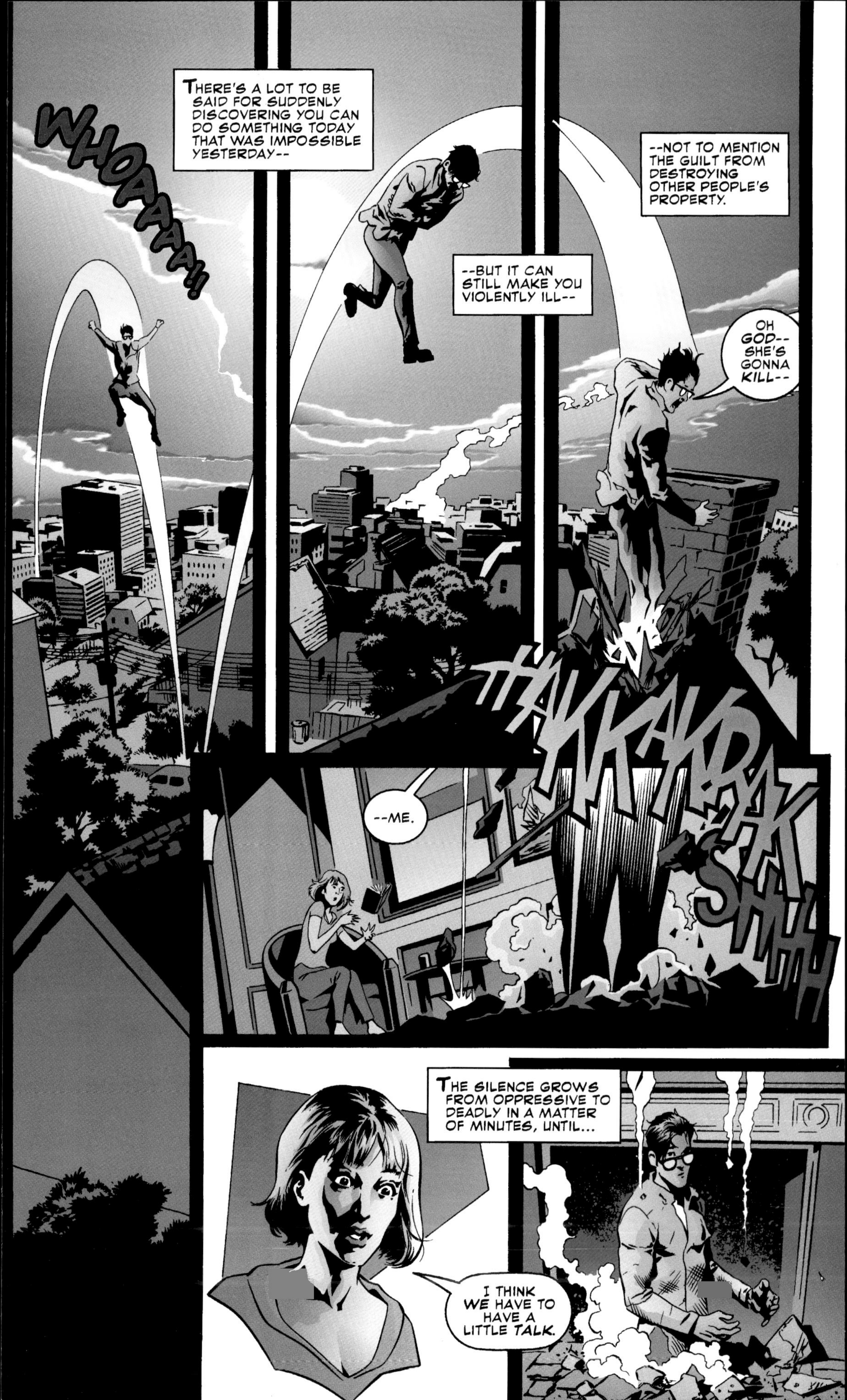
WHOAAAAA!!
THERE'S A LOT TO BE SAID FOR SUDDENLY DISCOVERING YOU CAN DO SOMETHING TODAY THAT WAS IMPOSSIBLE YESTERDAY--
--BUT IT CAN STILL MAKE YOU VIOLENTLY ILL--
--NOT TO MENTION THE GUILT FROM DESTROYING OTHER PEOPLE'S PROPERTY.
OH GOD--SHE'S GONNA KILL--
THAKKAKRAK
--ME.
SHHH
THE SILENCE GROWS FROM OPPRESSIVE TO DEADLY IN A MATTER OF MINUTES, UNTIL...
I THINK WE HAVE TO HAVE A LITTLE TALK.

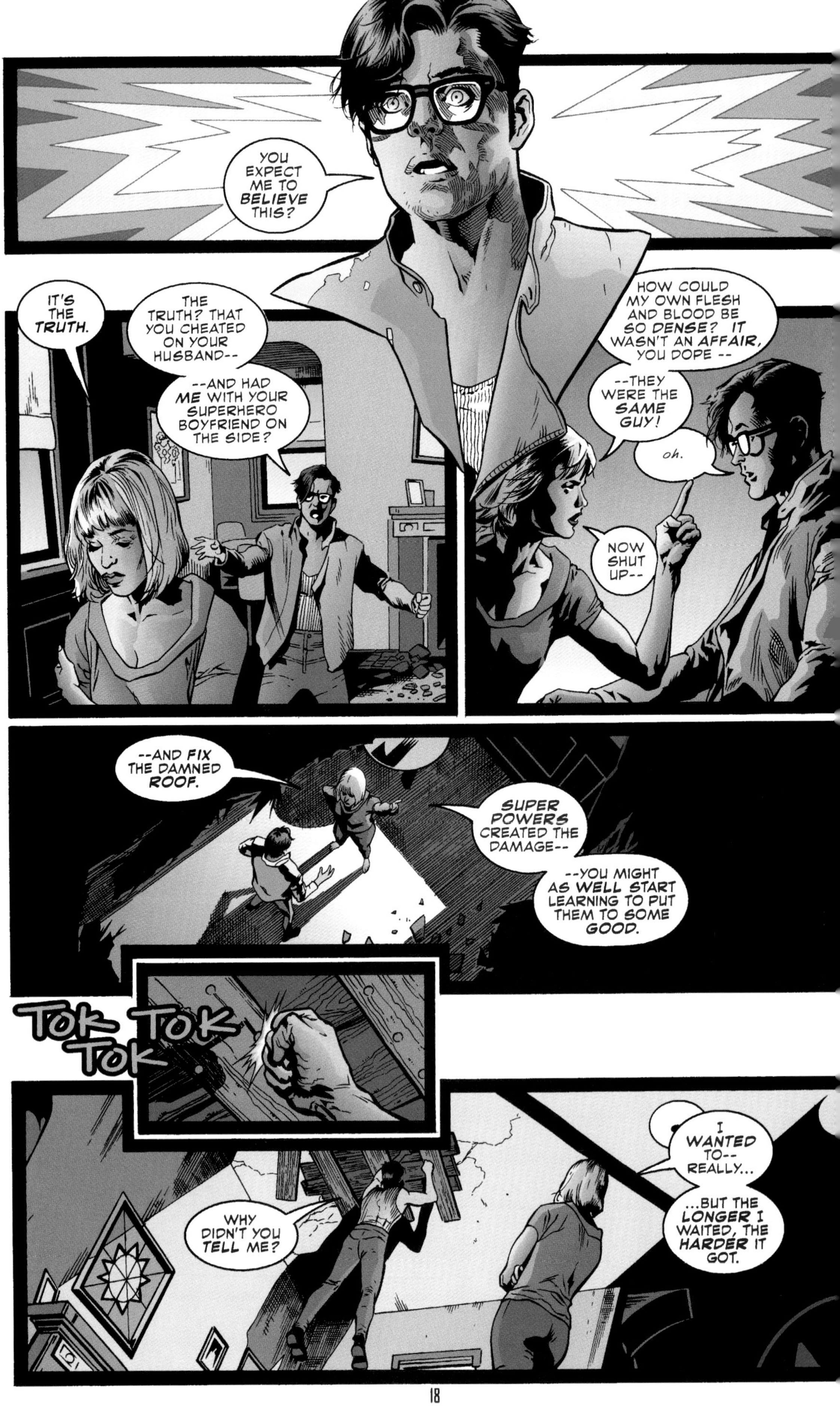
YOU EXPECT ME TO BELIEVE THIS?
IT'S THE TRUTH.
THE TRUTH? THAT YOU CHEATED ON YOUR HUSBAND--
--AND HAD ME WITH YOUR SUPERHERO BOYFRIEND ON THE SIDE?
HOW COULD MY OWN FLESH AND BLOOD BE SO DENSE? IT WASN'T AN AFFAIR, YOU DOPE --
--THEY WERE THE SAME GUY!
oh.
NOW SHUT UP--
--AND FIX THE DAMNED ROOF.
SUPER POWERS CREATED THE DAMAGE--
--YOU MIGHT AS WELL START LEARNING TO PUT THEM TO SOME GOOD.
TOK TOK TOK
WHY DIDN'T YOU TELL ME?
I WANTED TO-- REALLY...
...BUT THE LONGER I WAITED, THE HARDER IT GOT.

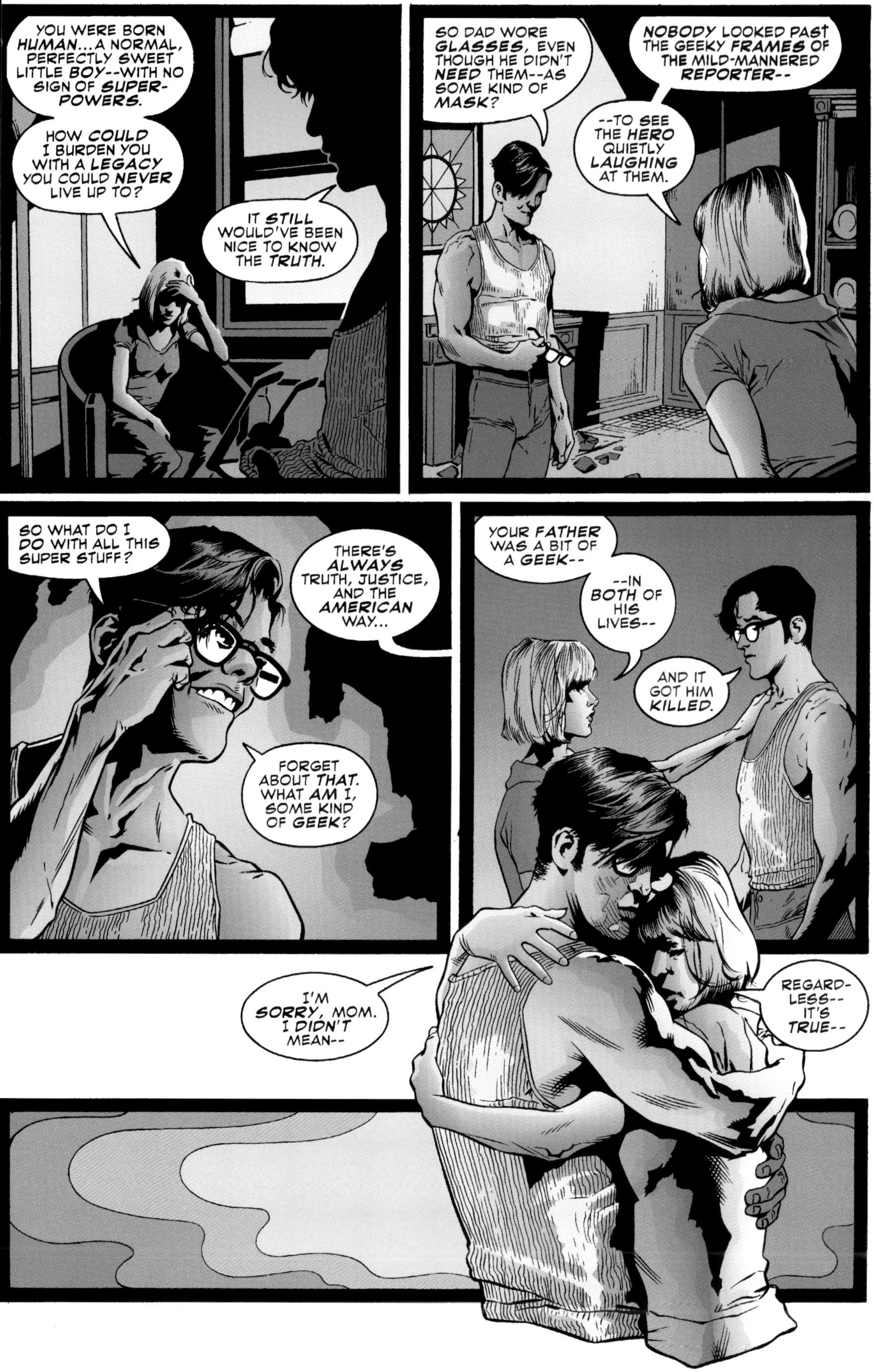
YOU WERE BORN HUMAN...A NORMAL, PERFECTLY SWEET LITTLE BOY--WITH NO SIGN OF SUPER-POWERS.
HOW COULD I BURDEN YOU WITH A LEGACY YOU COULD NEVER LIVE UP TO?
IT STILL WOULD'VE BEEN NICE TO KNOW THE TRUTH.
SO DAD WORE GLASSES, EVEN THOUGH HE DIDN'T NEED THEM--AS SOME KIND OF MASK?
NOBODY LOOKED PAST THE GEEKY FRAMES OF THE MILD-MANNERED REPORTER--
--TO SEE THE HERO QUIETLY LAUGHING AT THEM.
SO WHAT DO I DO WITH ALL THIS SUPER STUFF?
THERE'S ALWAYS TRUTH, JUSTICE, AND THE AMERICAN WAY...
FORGET ABOUT THAT. WHAT AM I, SOME KIND OF GEEK?
YOUR FATHER WAS A BIT OF A GEEK--
--IN BOTH OF HIS LIVES--
AND IT GOT HIM KILLED.
I'M SORRY, MOM. I DIDN'T MEAN--
REGARD-LESS--IT'S TRUE--

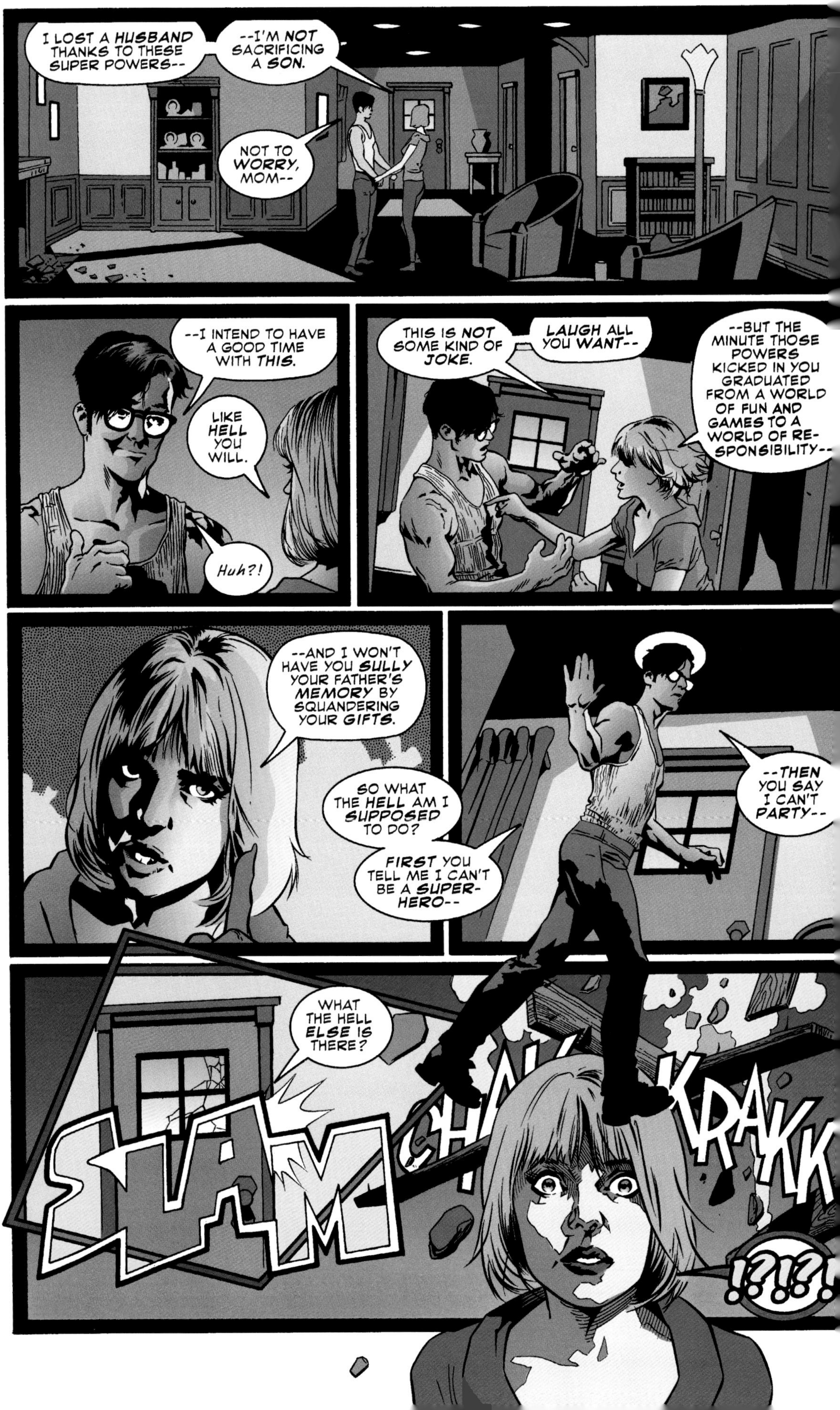
I LOST A HUSBAND THANKS TO THESE SUPER POWERS--
--I'M NOT SACRIFICING A SON.
NOT TO WORRY, MOM--
--I INTEND TO HAVE A GOOD TIME WITH THIS.
LIKE HELL YOU WILL.
Huh?!
THIS IS NOT SOME KIND OF JOKE.
LAUGH ALL YOU WANT--
--BUT THE MINUTE THOSE POWERS KICKED IN YOU GRADUATED FROM A WORLD OF FUN AND GAMES TO A WORLD OF RE-SPONSIBILITY--
--AND I WON'T HAVE YOU SULLY YOUR FATHER'S MEMORY BY SQUANDERING YOUR GIFTS.
SO WHAT THE HELL AM I SUPPOSED TO DO?
FIRST YOU TELL ME I CAN'T BE A SUPER-HERO--
--THEN YOU SAY I CAN'T PARTY--
WHAT THE HELL ELSE IS THERE?
SLAM
KRAKK
!?!?!

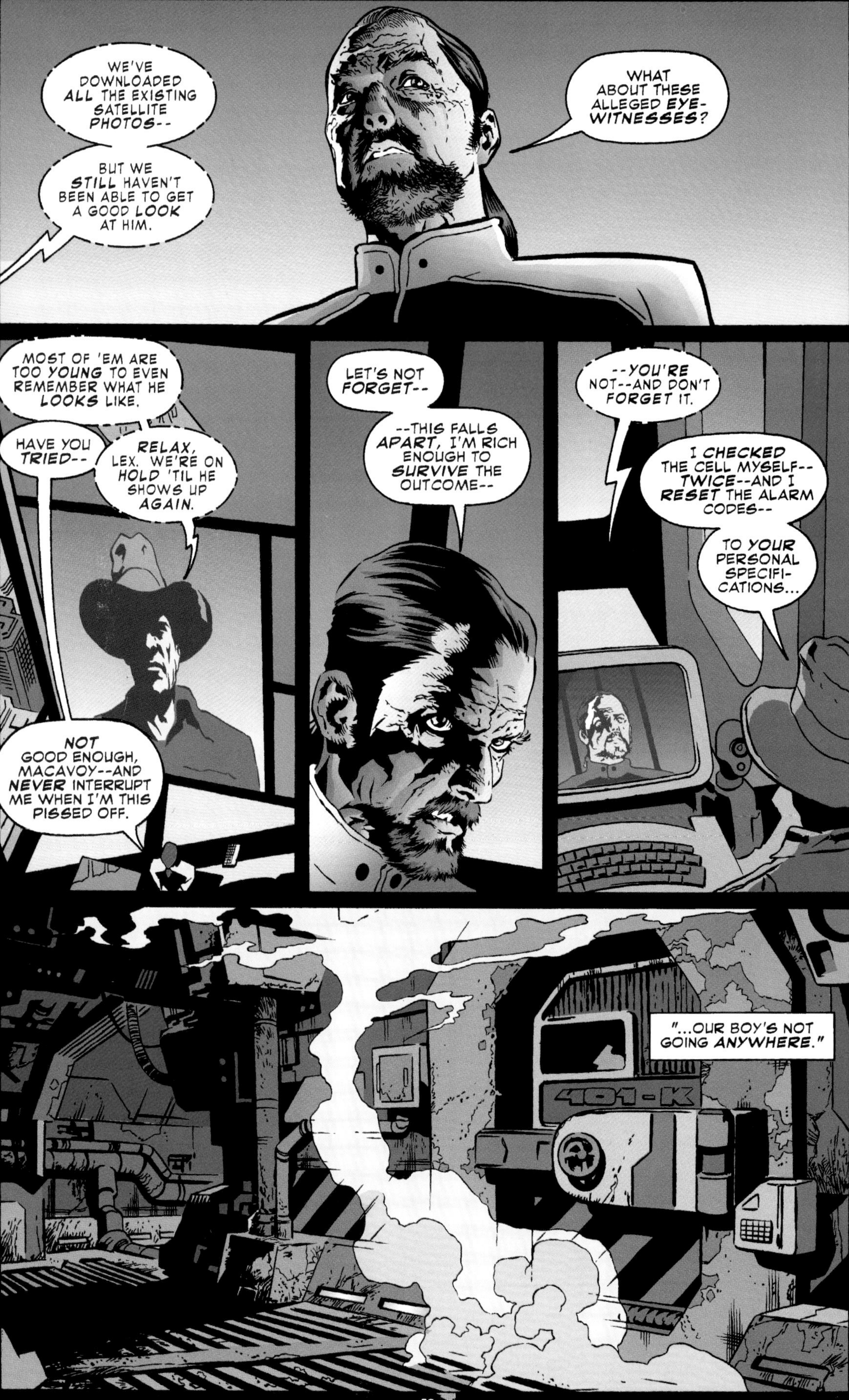
WE'VE DOWNLOADED ALL THE EXISTING SATELLITE PHOTOS--
BUT WE STILL HAVEN'T BEEN ABLE TO GET A GOOD LOOK AT HIM.
WHAT ABOUT THESE ALLEGED EYE-WITNESSES?
MOST OF 'EM ARE TOO YOUNG TO EVEN REMEMBER WHAT HE LOOKS LIKE.
HAVE YOU TRIED--
RELAX, LEX. WE'RE ON HOLD 'TIL HE SHOWS UP AGAIN.
NOT GOOD ENOUGH, MACAVOY--AND NEVER INTERRUPT ME WHEN I'M THIS PISSED OFF.
LET'S NOT FORGET--
--THIS FALLS APART, I'M RICH ENOUGH TO SURVIVE THE OUTCOME--
--YOU'RE NOT--AND DON'T FORGET IT.
I CHECKED THE CELL MYSELF--TWICE--AND I RESET THE ALARM CODES--
TO YOUR PERSONAL SPECIFI-CATIONS...
"...OUR BOY'S NOT GOING ANYWHERE."
401-K

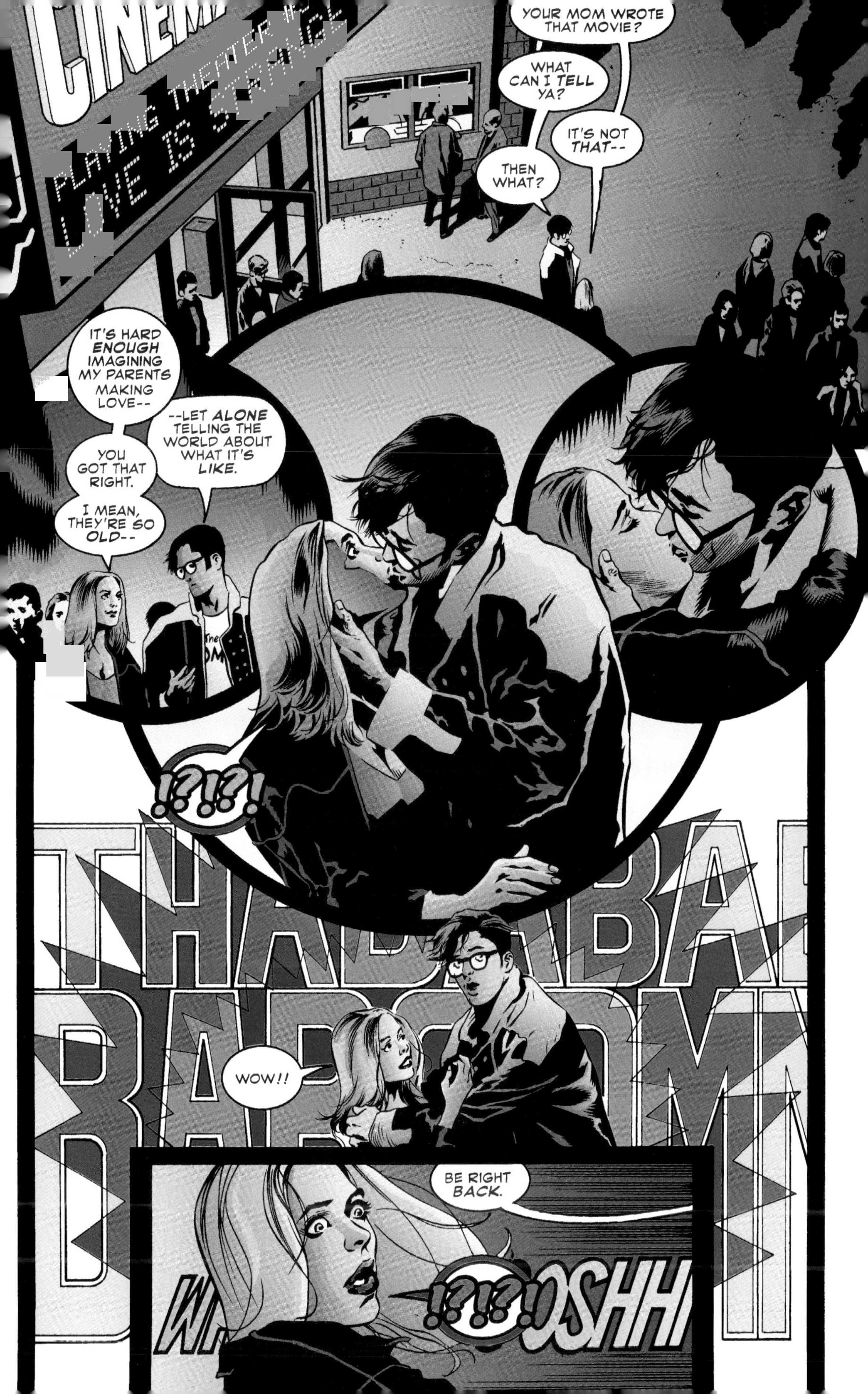
YOUR MOM WROTE THAT MOVIE?
WHAT CAN I TELL YA?
IT'S NOT THAT--
THEN WHAT?
IT'S HARD ENOUGH IMAGINING MY PARENTS MAKING LOVE--
--LET ALONE TELLING THE WORLD ABOUT WHAT IT'S LIKE.
YOU GOT THAT RIGHT.
I MEAN, THEY'RE SO OLD--
!?!?!
WOW!!
BE RIGHT BACK.
!?!?!

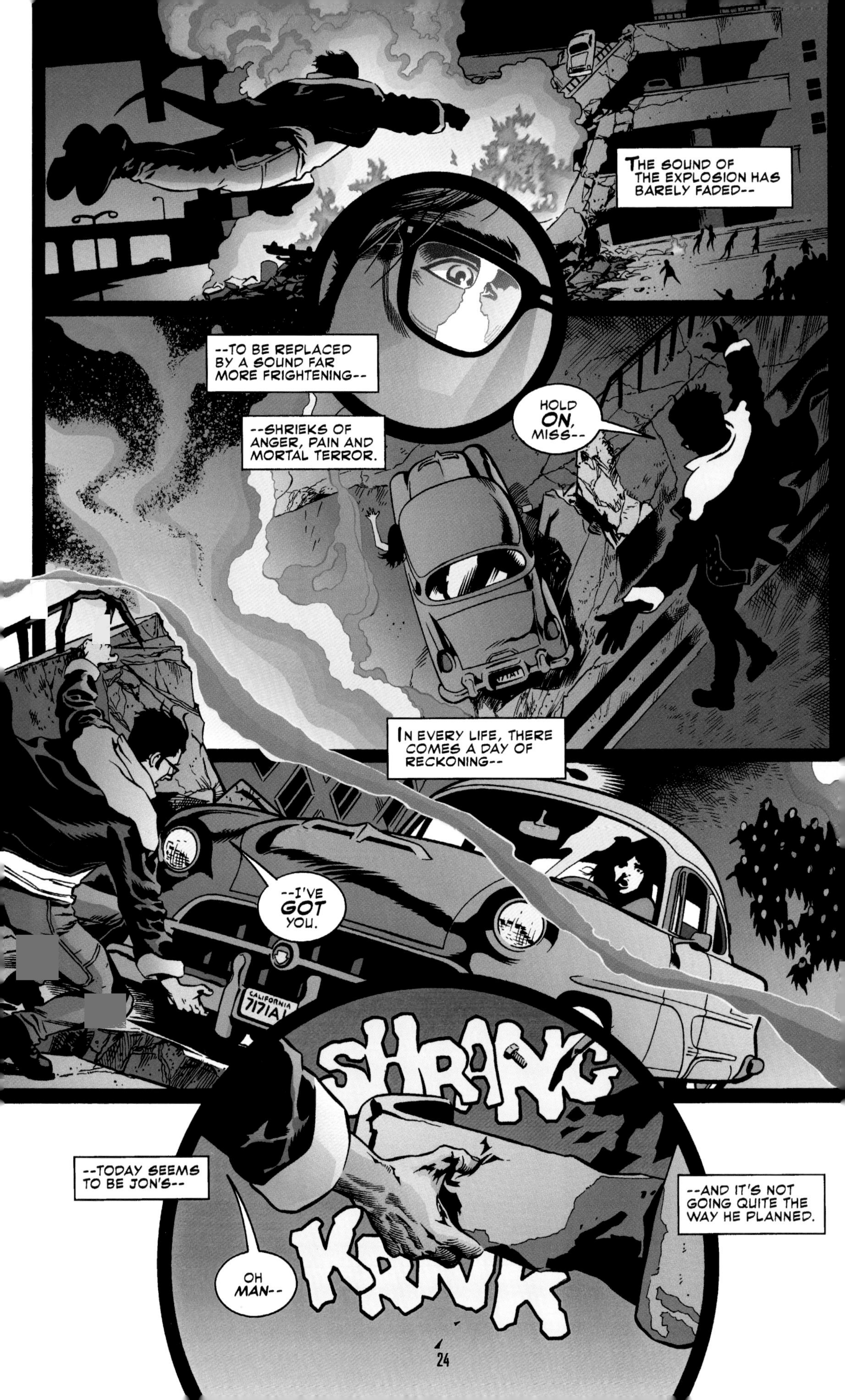
THE SOUND OF THE EXPLOSION HAS BARELY FADED--
--TO BE REPLACED BY A SOUND FAR MORE FRIGHTENING--
--SHRIEKS OF ANGER, PAIN AND MORTAL TERROR.
HOLD ON, MISS--
IN EVERY LIFE, THERE COMES A DAY OF RECKONING--
--I'VE GOT YOU.
CALIFORNIA
7171AL
SHRANG
--TODAY SEEMS TO BE JON'S--
--AND IT'S NOT GOING QUITE THE WAY HE PLANNED.
OH MAN--
KRNK

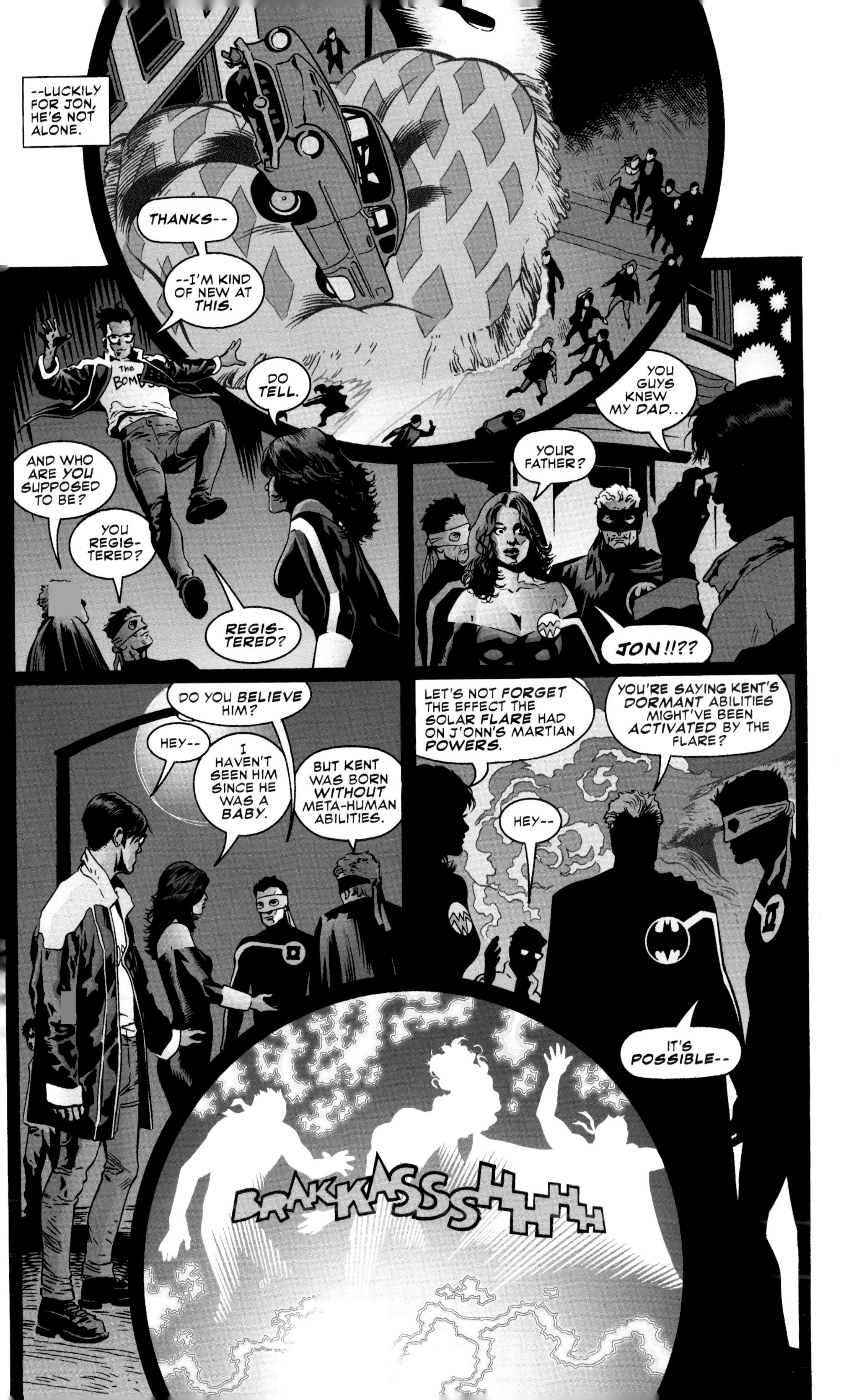
--LUCKILY FOR JON, HE'S NOT ALONE.
THANKS--
--I'M KIND OF NEW AT THIS.
DO TELL.
AND WHO ARE YOU SUPPOSED TO BE?
YOU REGIS-TERED?
REGIS-TERED?
YOU GUYS KNEW MY DAD...
YOUR FATHER?
JON!!??
DO YOU BELIEVE HIM?
HEY--
I HAVEN'T SEEN HIM SINCE HE WAS A BABY.
BUT KENT WAS BORN WITHOUT META-HUMAN ABILITIES.
LET'S NOT FORGET THE EFFECT THE SOLAR FLARE HAD ON J'ONN'S MARTIAN POWERS.
YOU'RE SAYING KENT'S DORMANT ABILITIES MIGHT'VE BEEN ACTIVATED BY THE FLARE?
HEY--
IT'S POSSIBLE--
BRAKKASSSHHHH

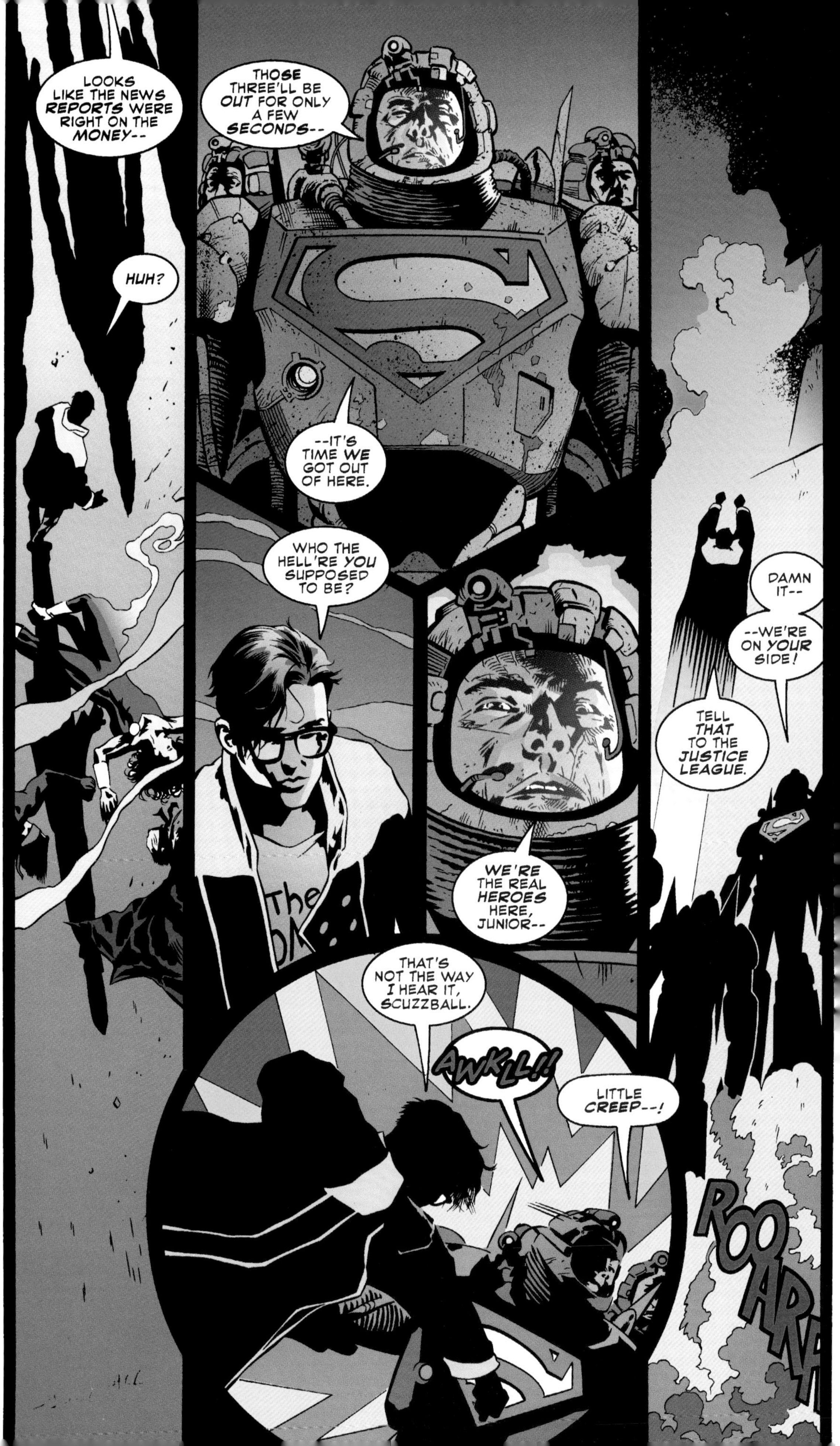
LOOKS LIKE THE NEWS REPORTS WERE RIGHT ON THE MONEY--
THOSE THREE'LL BE OUT FOR ONLY A FEW SECONDS--
HUH?
--IT'S TIME WE GOT OUT OF HERE.
WHO THE HELL'RE YOU SUPPOSED TO BE?
WE'RE THE REAL HEROES HERE, JUNIOR--
DAMN IT--
--WE'RE ON YOUR SIDE!
TELL THAT TO THE JUSTICE LEAGUE.
THAT'S NOT THE WAY I HEAR IT, SCUZZBALL.
AWKLL!!
LITTLE CREEP--!
ROOARR

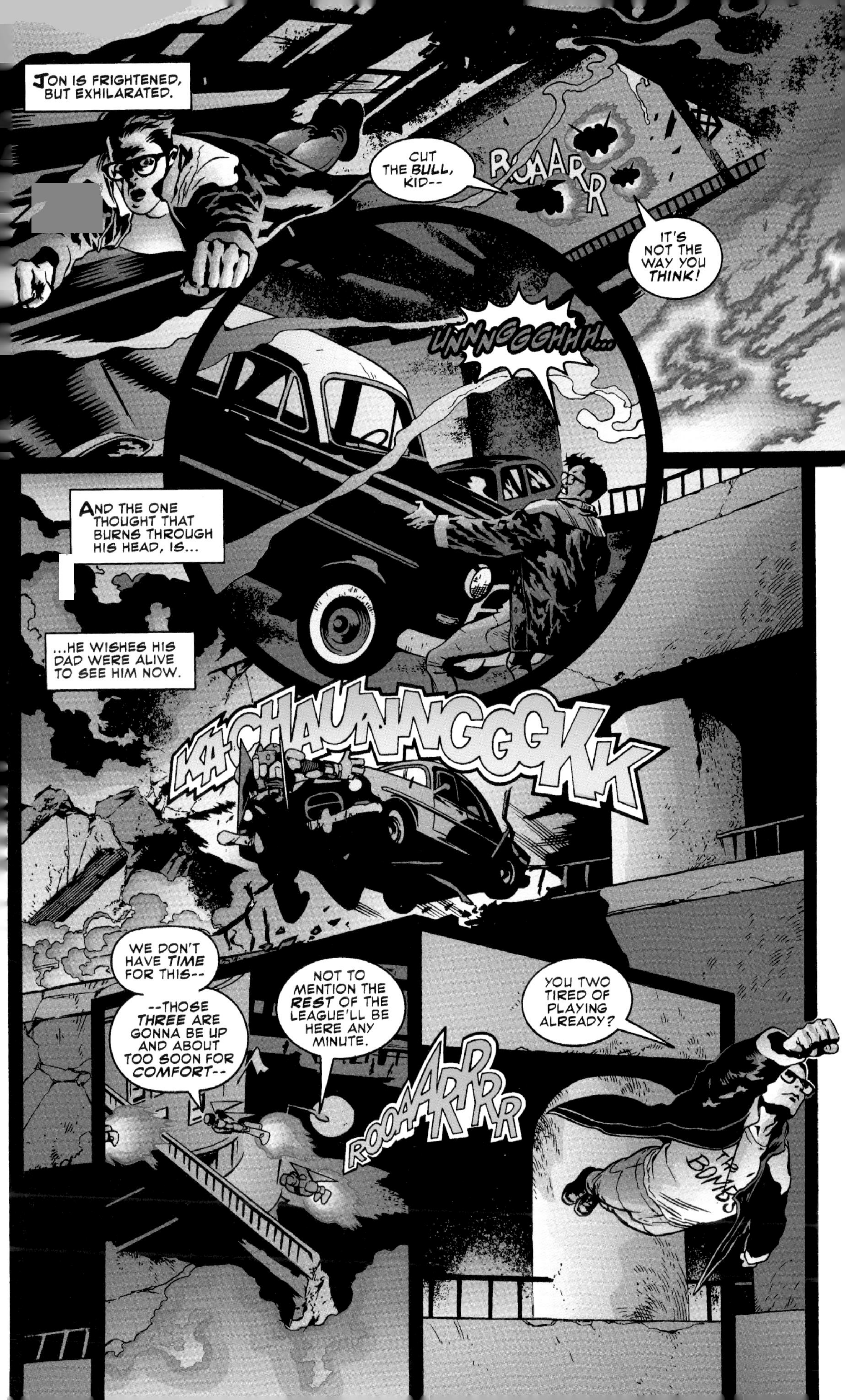
JON IS FRIGHTENED, BUT EXHILARATED.
CUT THE **BULL**, KID--
ROAARR
IT'S NOT THE WAY YOU *THINK!*
UNNNGGGHHH...
AND THE ONE THOUGHT THAT BURNS THROUGH HIS HEAD, IS...
...HE WISHES HIS DAD WERE ALIVE TO SEE HIM NOW.
KACHAUNNGGGKK
WE DON'T HAVE *TIME* FOR THIS--
--THOSE *THREE* ARE GONNA BE UP AND ABOUT TOO SOON FOR *COMFORT*--
NOT TO MENTION THE *REST* OF THE LEAGUE'LL BE HERE ANY MINUTE.
YOU TWO TIRED OF PLAYING ALREADY?
ROOAARRRR

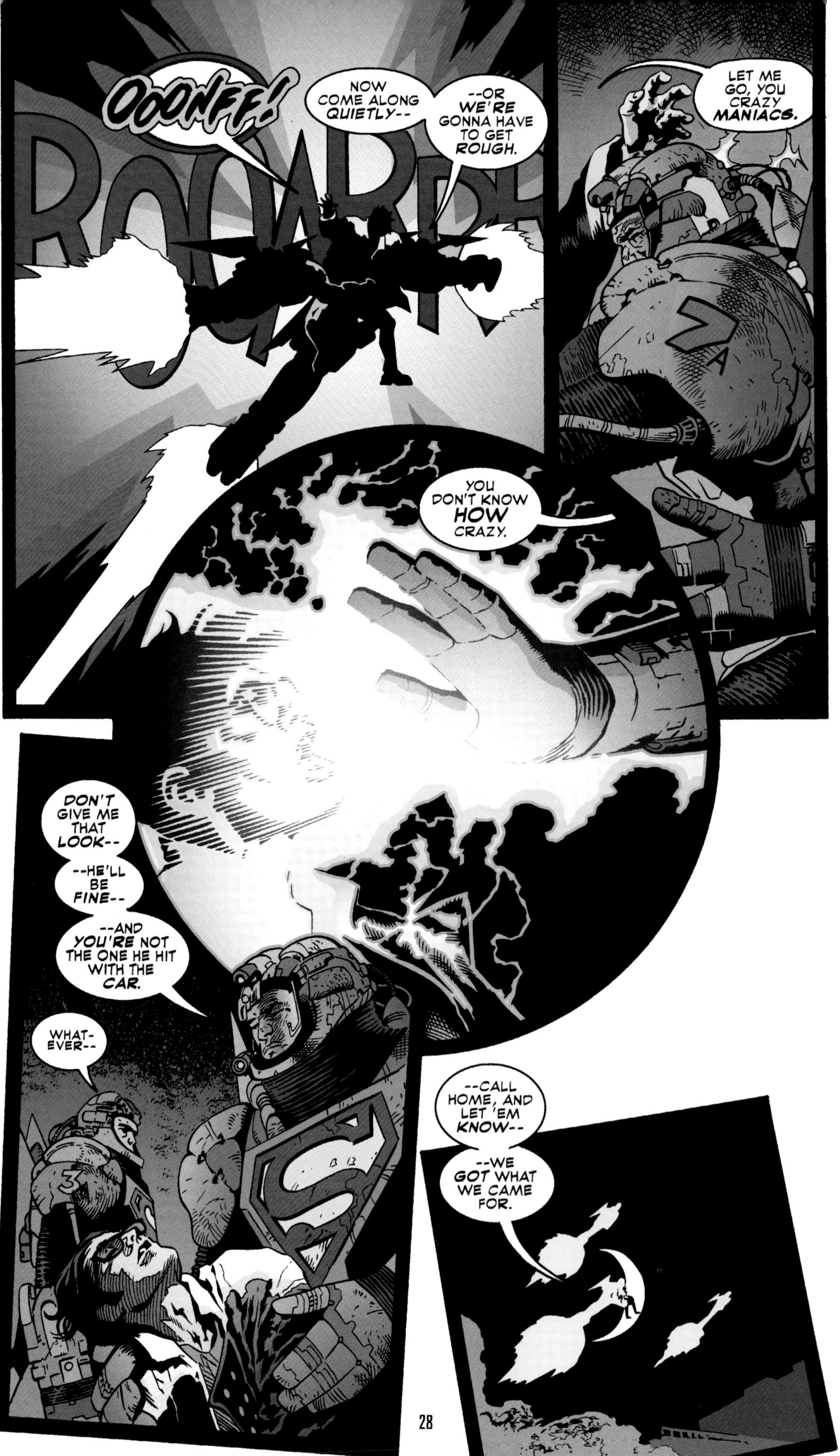
OOONFF!
ROOARRR
NOW COME ALONG QUIETLY--
--OR WE'RE GONNA HAVE TO GET ROUGH.
LET ME GO, YOU CRAZY MANIACS.
YOU DON'T KNOW HOW CRAZY.
DON'T GIVE ME THAT LOOK--
--HE'LL BE FINE--
--AND YOU'RE NOT THE ONE HE HIT WITH THE CAR.
WHAT-EVER--
--CALL HOME, AND LET 'EM KNOW--
--WE GOT WHAT WE CAME FOR.

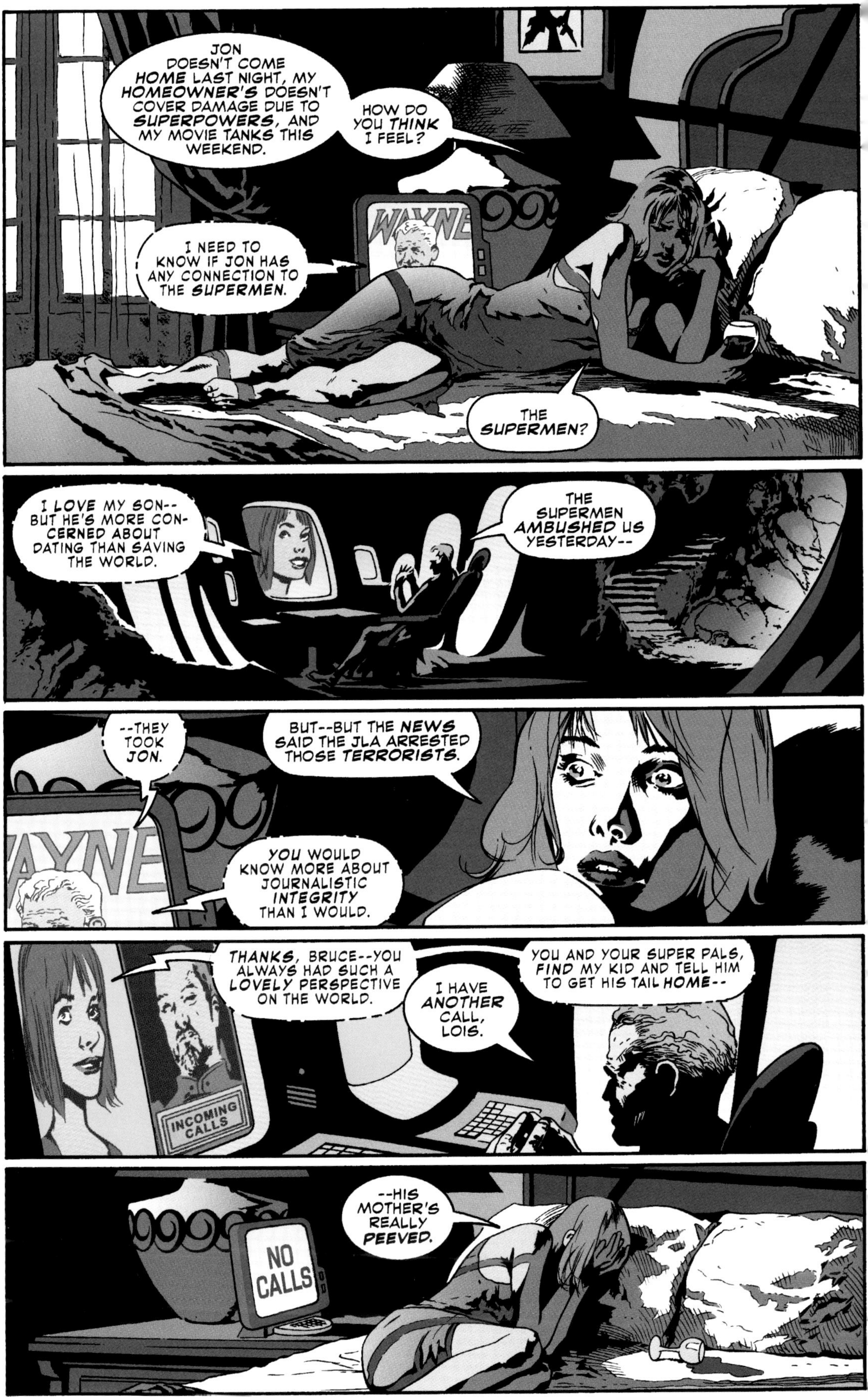
JON DOESN'T COME HOME LAST NIGHT, MY HOMEOWNER'S DOESN'T COVER DAMAGE DUE TO SUPERPOWERS, AND MY MOVIE TANKS THIS WEEKEND.
HOW DO YOU THINK I FEEL?
WAYNE
I NEED TO KNOW IF JON HAS ANY CONNECTION TO THE SUPERMEN.
THE SUPERMEN?
I LOVE MY SON--BUT HE'S MORE CON-CERNED ABOUT DATING THAN SAVING THE WORLD.
THE SUPERMEN AMBUSHED US YESTERDAY--
--THEY TOOK JON.
BUT--BUT THE NEWS SAID THE JLA ARRESTED THOSE TERRORISTS.
YOU WOULD KNOW MORE ABOUT JOURNALISTIC INTEGRITY THAN I WOULD.
THANKS, BRUCE--YOU ALWAYS HAD SUCH A LOVELY PERSPECTIVE ON THE WORLD.
YOU AND YOUR SUPER PALS, FIND MY KID AND TELL HIM TO GET HIS TAIL HOME--
I HAVE ANOTHER CALL, LOIS.
INCOMING CALLS
--HIS MOTHER'S REALLY PEEVED.
NO CALLS

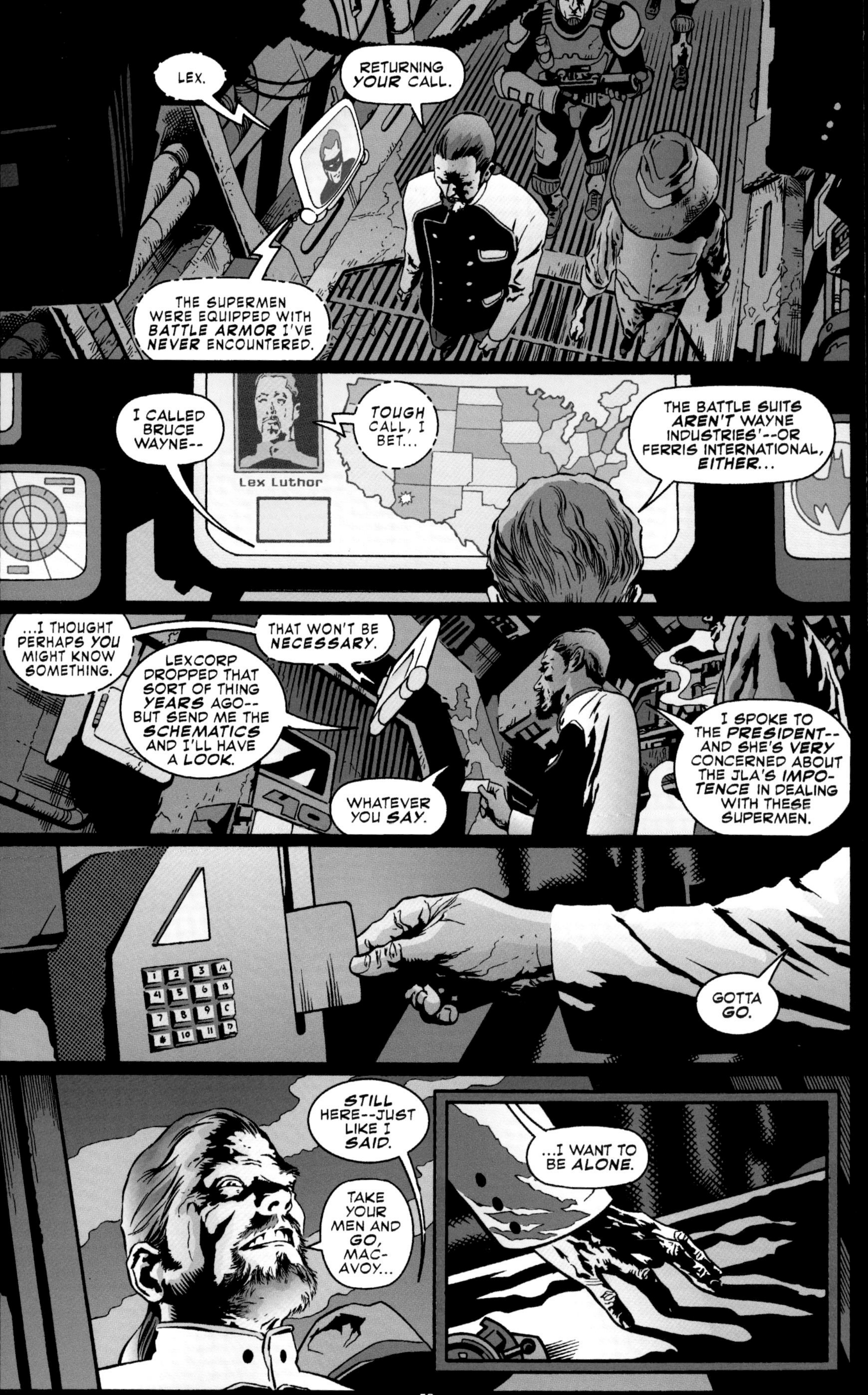
LEX.
RETURNING YOUR CALL.
THE SUPERMEN WERE EQUIPPED WITH BATTLE ARMOR I'VE NEVER ENCOUNTERED.
I CALLED BRUCE WAYNE--
TOUGH CALL, I BET...
Lex Luthor
THE BATTLE SUITS AREN'T WAYNE INDUSTRIES'--OR FERRIS INTERNATIONAL, EITHER...
...I THOUGHT PERHAPS YOU MIGHT KNOW SOMETHING.
THAT WON'T BE NECESSARY.
LEXCORP DROPPED THAT SORT OF THING YEARS AGO--BUT SEND ME THE SCHEMATICS AND I'LL HAVE A LOOK.
WHATEVER YOU SAY.
I SPOKE TO THE PRESIDENT--AND SHE'S VERY CONCERNED ABOUT THE JLA'S IMPOTENCE IN DEALING WITH THESE SUPERMEN.
GOTTA GO.
STILL HERE--JUST LIKE I SAID.
TAKE YOUR MEN AND GO, MACAVOY...
...I WANT TO BE ALONE.

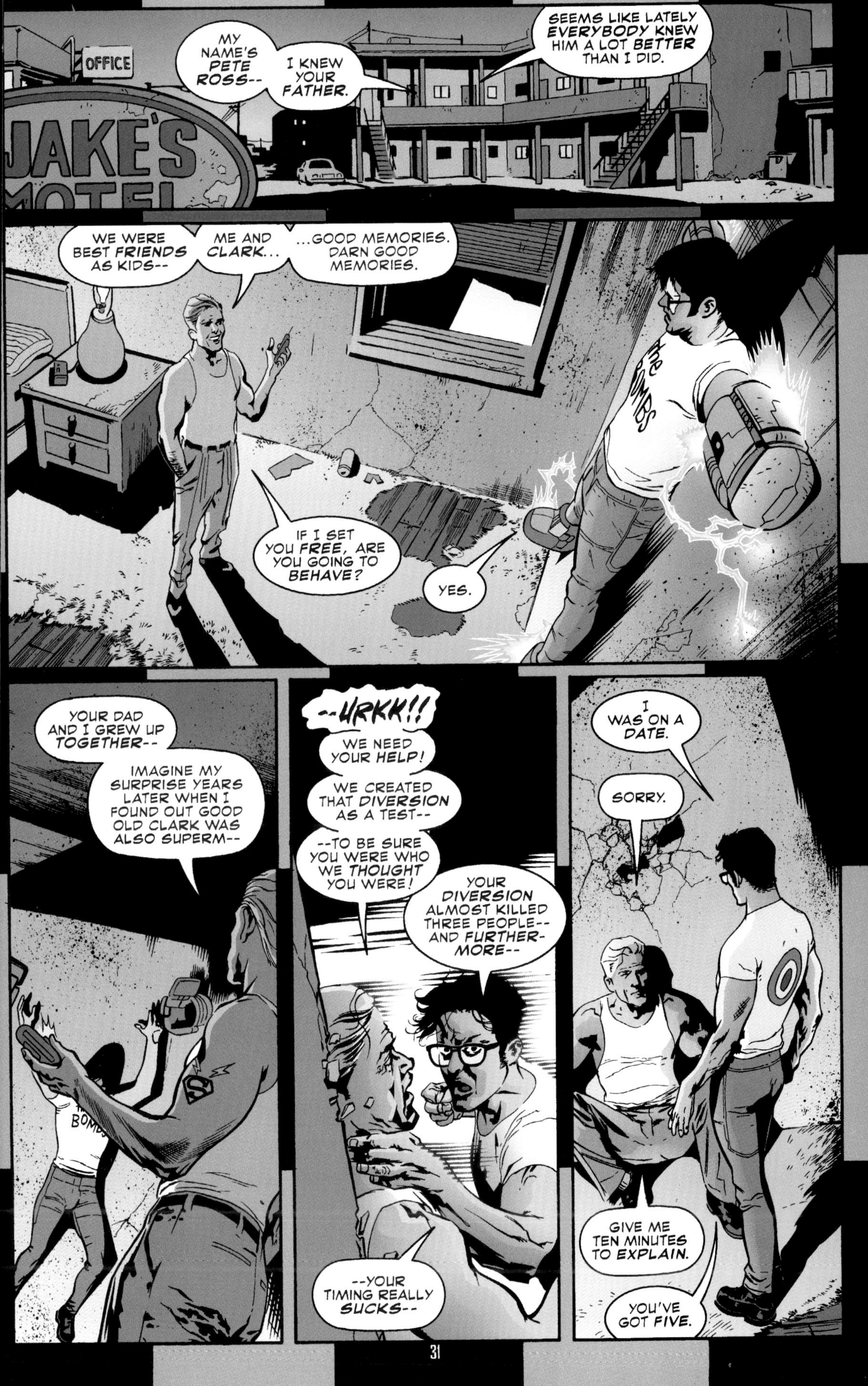
OFFICE
JAKE'S MOTEL
MY NAME'S PETE ROSS--
I KNEW YOUR FATHER.
SEEMS LIKE LATELY EVERYBODY KNEW HIM A LOT BETTER THAN I DID.
WE WERE BEST FRIENDS AS KIDS--
ME AND CLARK...
...GOOD MEMORIES. DARN GOOD MEMORIES.
THE BOMBS
IF I SET YOU FREE, ARE YOU GOING TO BEHAVE?
YES.
YOUR DAD AND I GREW UP TOGETHER--
IMAGINE MY SURPRISE YEARS LATER WHEN I FOUND OUT GOOD OLD CLARK WAS ALSO SUPERM--
--URKK!!
WE NEED YOUR HELP!
WE CREATED THAT DIVERSION AS A TEST--
--TO BE SURE YOU WERE WHO WE THOUGHT YOU WERE!
YOUR DIVERSION ALMOST KILLED THREE PEOPLE--AND FURTHER-MORE--
--YOUR TIMING REALLY SUCKS--
I WAS ON A DATE.
SORRY.
GIVE ME TEN MINUTES TO EXPLAIN.
YOU'VE GOT FIVE.

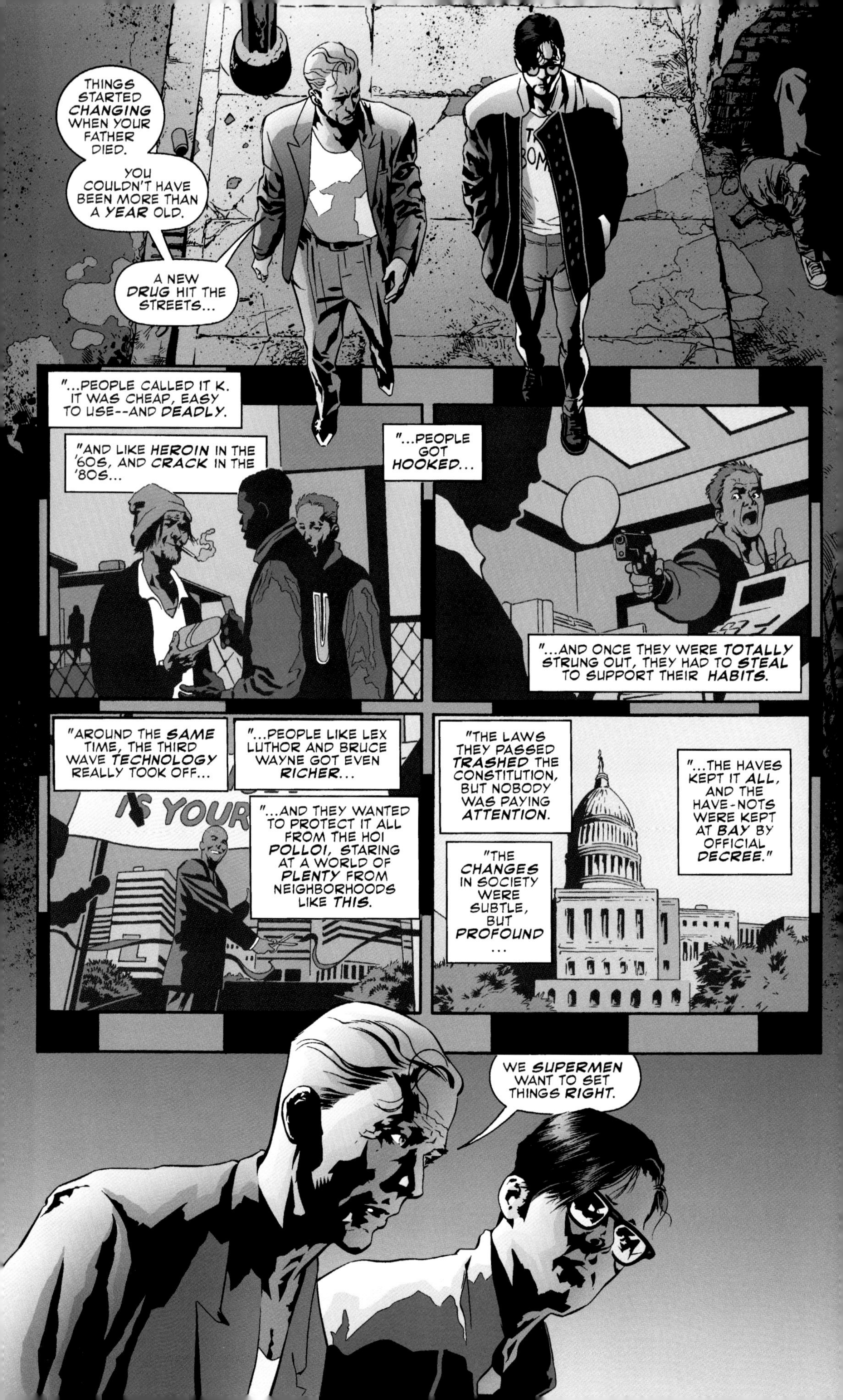

THINGS STARTED CHANGING WHEN YOUR FATHER DIED.
YOU COULDN'T HAVE BEEN MORE THAN A YEAR OLD.
A NEW DRUG HIT THE STREETS...
"...PEOPLE CALLED IT K. IT WAS CHEAP, EASY TO USE--AND DEADLY.
"AND LIKE HEROIN IN THE '60S, AND CRACK IN THE '80S...
"...PEOPLE GOT HOOKED...
"...AND ONCE THEY WERE TOTALLY STRUNG OUT, THEY HAD TO STEAL TO SUPPORT THEIR HABITS.
"AROUND THE SAME TIME, THE THIRD WAVE TECHNOLOGY REALLY TOOK OFF...
"...PEOPLE LIKE LEX LUTHOR AND BRUCE WAYNE GOT EVEN RICHER...
"...AND THEY WANTED TO PROTECT IT ALL FROM THE HOI POLLOI, STARING AT A WORLD OF PLENTY FROM NEIGHBORHOODS LIKE THIS.
IS YOUR
"THE LAWS THEY PASSED TRASHED THE CONSTITUTION, BUT NOBODY WAS PAYING ATTENTION.
"THE CHANGES IN SOCIETY WERE SUBTLE, BUT PROFOUND...
"...THE HAVES KEPT IT ALL, AND THE HAVE-NOTS WERE KEPT AT BAY BY OFFICIAL DECREE."
WE SUPERMEN WANT TO SET THINGS RIGHT.

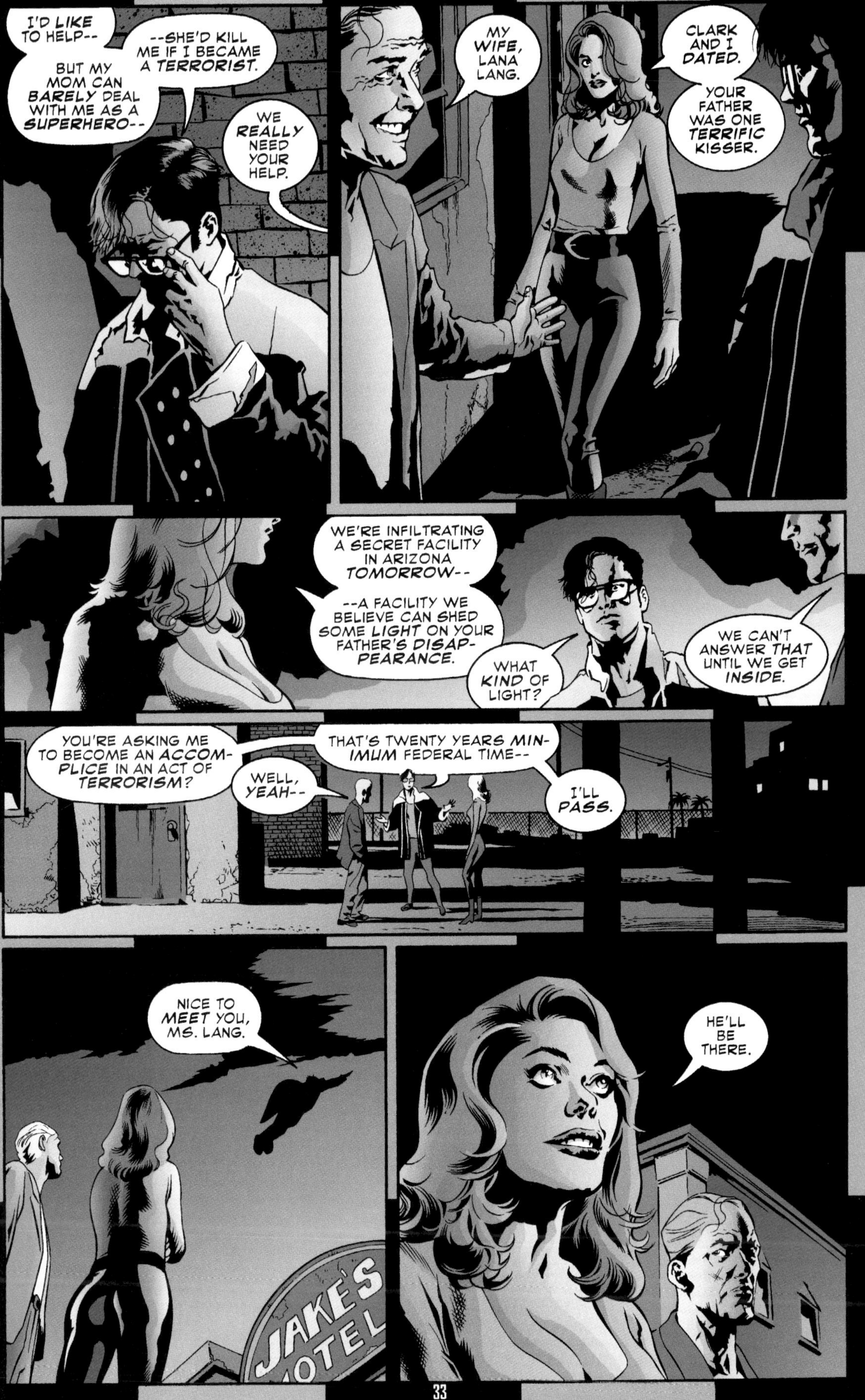

I'D LIKE TO HELP--
BUT MY MOM CAN BARELY DEAL WITH ME AS A SUPERHERO--
--SHE'D KILL ME IF I BECAME A TERRORIST.
WE REALLY NEED YOUR HELP.
MY WIFE, LANA LANG.
CLARK AND I DATED.
YOUR FATHER WAS ONE TERRIFIC KISSER.
WE'RE INFILTRATING A SECRET FACILITY IN ARIZONA TOMORROW--
--A FACILITY WE BELIEVE CAN SHED SOME LIGHT ON YOUR FATHER'S DISAP-PEARANCE.
WHAT KIND OF LIGHT?
WE CAN'T ANSWER THAT UNTIL WE GET INSIDE.
YOU'RE ASKING ME TO BECOME AN ACCOM-PLICE IN AN ACT OF TERRORISM?
WELL, YEAH--
THAT'S TWENTY YEARS MIN-IMUM FEDERAL TIME--
I'LL PASS.
NICE TO MEET YOU, MS. LANG.
JAKE'S MOTEL
HE'LL BE THERE.

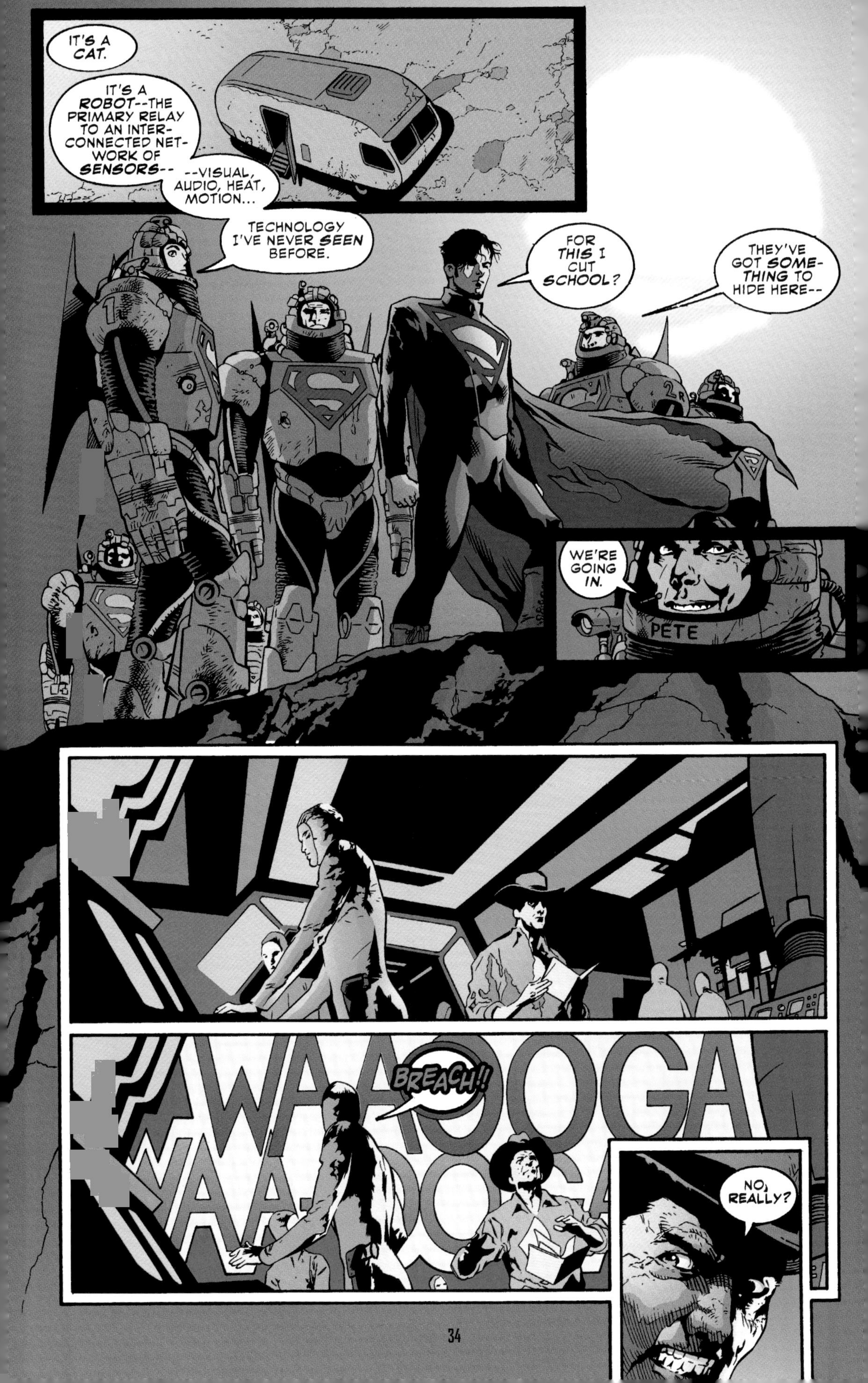
IT'S A CAT.
IT'S A ROBOT--THE PRIMARY RELAY TO AN INTER-CONNECTED NET-WORK OF SENSORS--
--VISUAL, AUDIO, HEAT, MOTION...
TECHNOLOGY I'VE NEVER SEEN BEFORE.
FOR THIS I CUT SCHOOL?
THEY'VE GOT SOME-THING TO HIDE HERE--
WE'RE GOING IN.
PETE
WAAOOGA
BREACH!!
NO, REALLY?

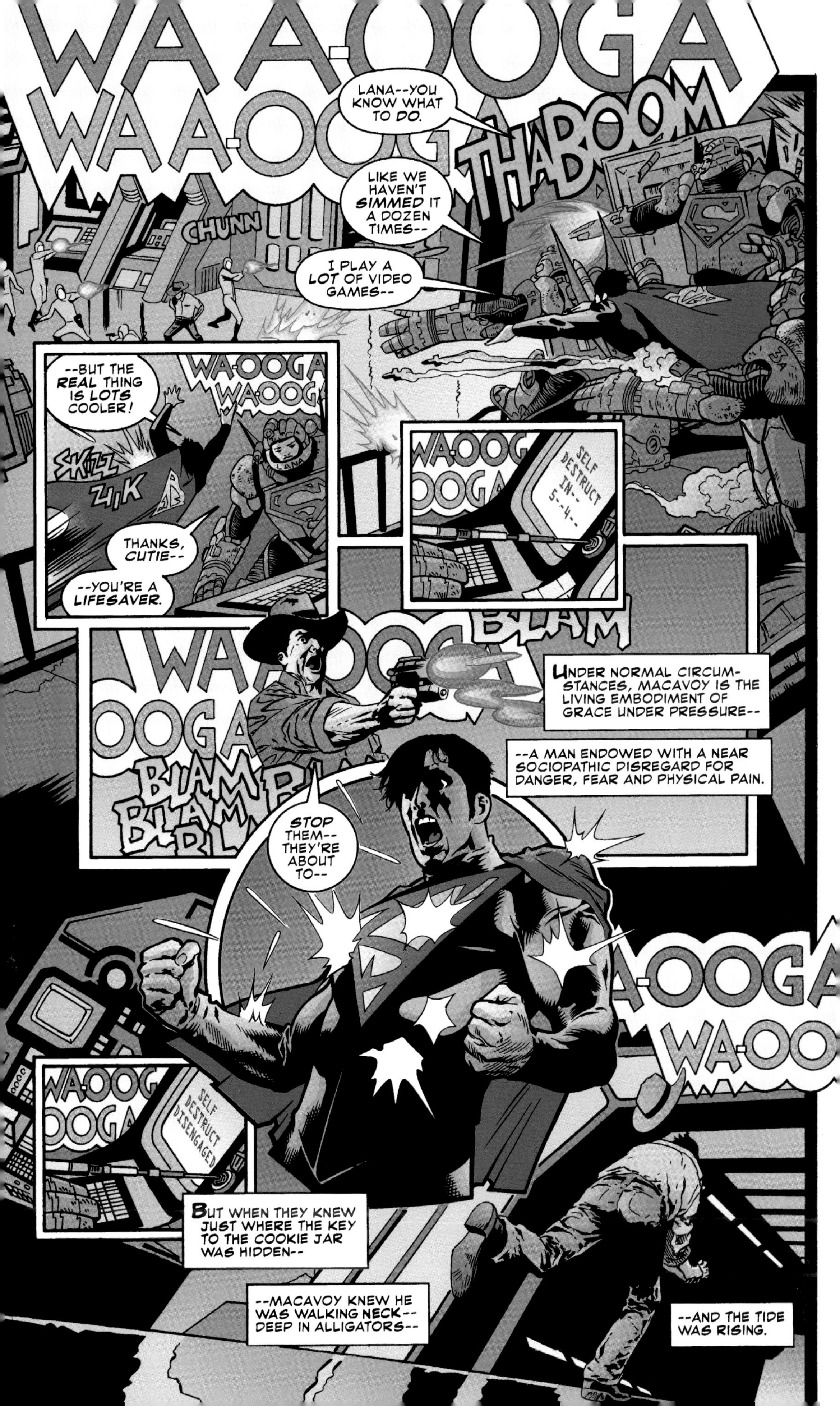

WA A-OOGA
WA A-OOGA
LANA--YOU KNOW WHAT TO DO.
THABOOM
LIKE WE HAVEN'T SIMMED IT A DOZEN TIMES--
CHUNN
I PLAY A LOT OF VIDEO GAMES--
--BUT THE REAL THING IS LOTS COOLER!
WA-OOGA
WA-OOG
SKZZZ
ZIK
LANA
THANKS, CUTIE--
--YOU'RE A LIFESAVER.
WA-OOG
OOGA
SELF DESTRUCT IN-- 5--4--
WA-OOGA
OOGA
BLAM
UNDER NORMAL CIRCUMSTANCES, MACAVOY IS THE LIVING EMBODIMENT OF GRACE UNDER PRESSURE--
--A MAN ENDOWED WITH A NEAR SOCIOPATHIC DISREGARD FOR DANGER, FEAR AND PHYSICAL PAIN.
BLAM
BLAM
STOP THEM--THEY'RE ABOUT TO--
A-OOGA
WA-OO
WA-OOG
OOGA
SELF DESTRUCT DISENGAGED
BUT WHEN THEY KNEW JUST WHERE THE KEY TO THE COOKIE JAR WAS HIDDEN--
--MACAVOY KNEW HE WAS WALKING NECK--DEEP IN ALLIGATORS--
--AND THE TIDE WAS RISING.

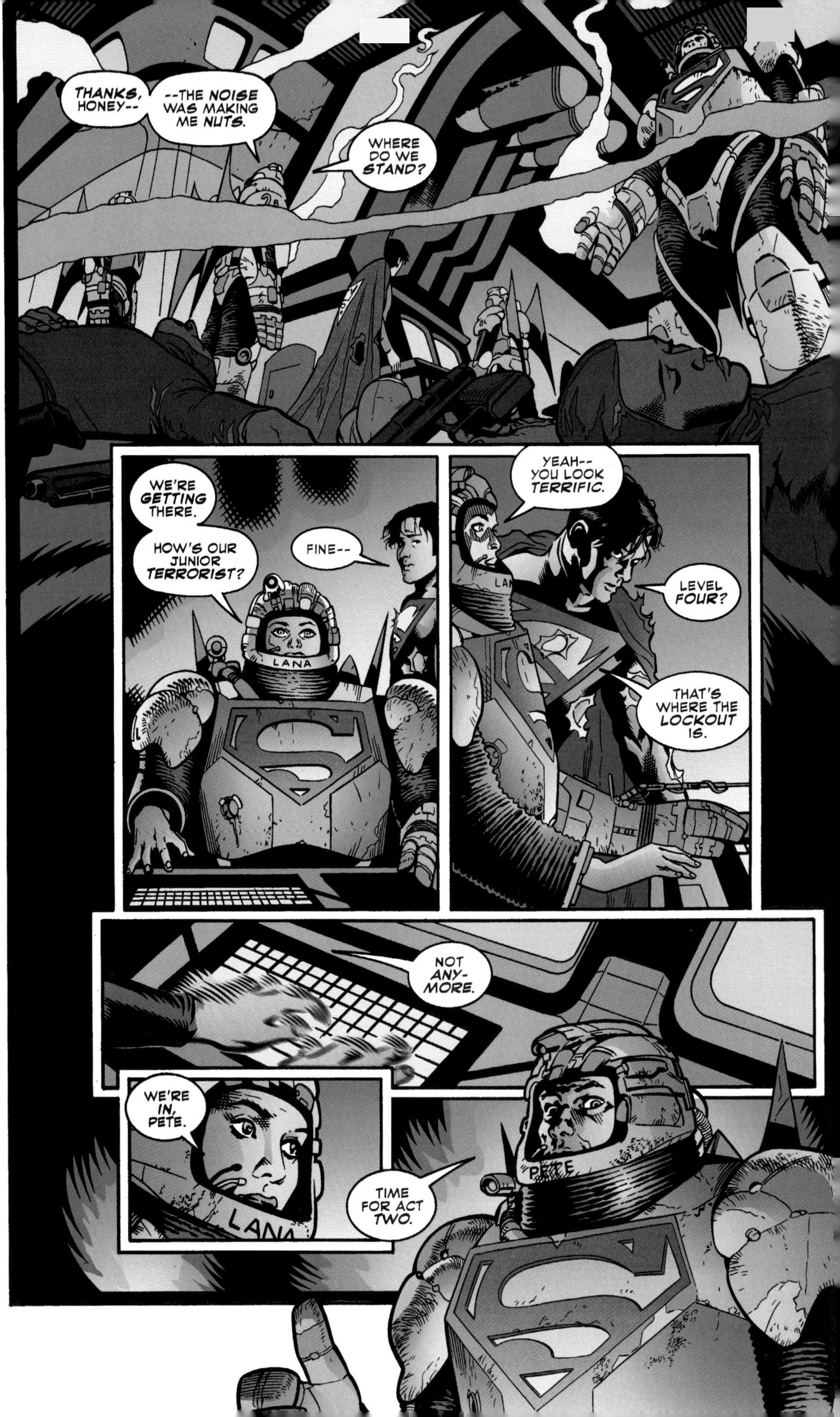
THANKS, HONEY--
--THE NOISE WAS MAKING ME NUTS.
WHERE DO WE STAND?
WE'RE GETTING THERE.
HOW'S OUR JUNIOR TERRORIST?
FINE--
LANA
YEAH-- YOU LOOK TERRIFIC.
LEVEL FOUR?
THAT'S WHERE THE LOCKOUT IS.
NOT ANY-MORE.
WE'RE IN, PETE.
LANA
PETE
TIME FOR ACT TWO.

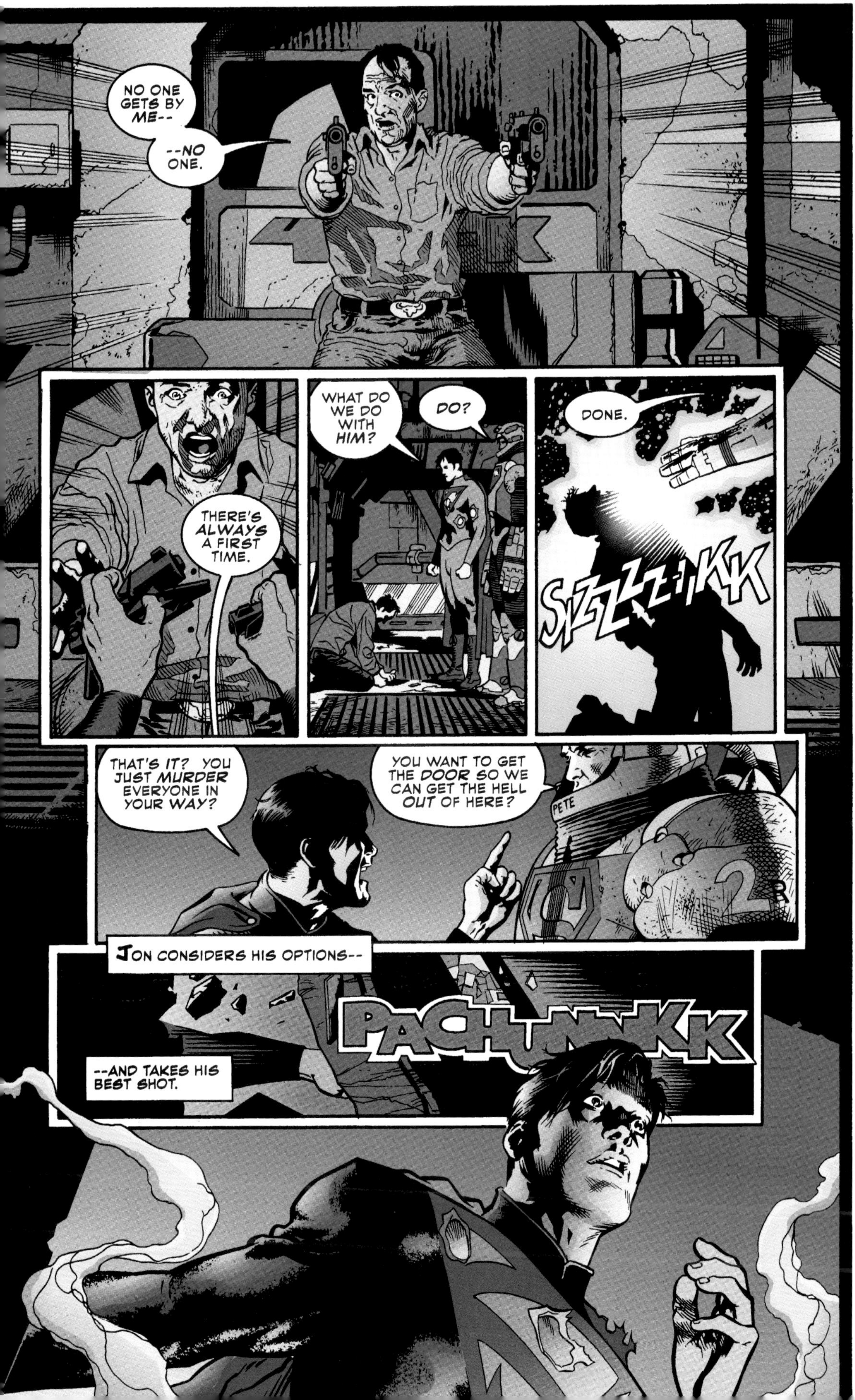
NO ONE GETS BY ME--
--NO ONE.
THERE'S ALWAYS A FIRST TIME.
WHAT DO WE DO WITH HIM?
DO?
DONE.
SIZZZZ-IKK
THAT'S IT? YOU JUST MURDER EVERYONE IN YOUR WAY?
YOU WANT TO GET THE DOOR SO WE CAN GET THE HELL OUT OF HERE?
PETE
JON CONSIDERS HIS OPTIONS--
PACHUNNKK
--AND TAKES HIS BEST SHOT.

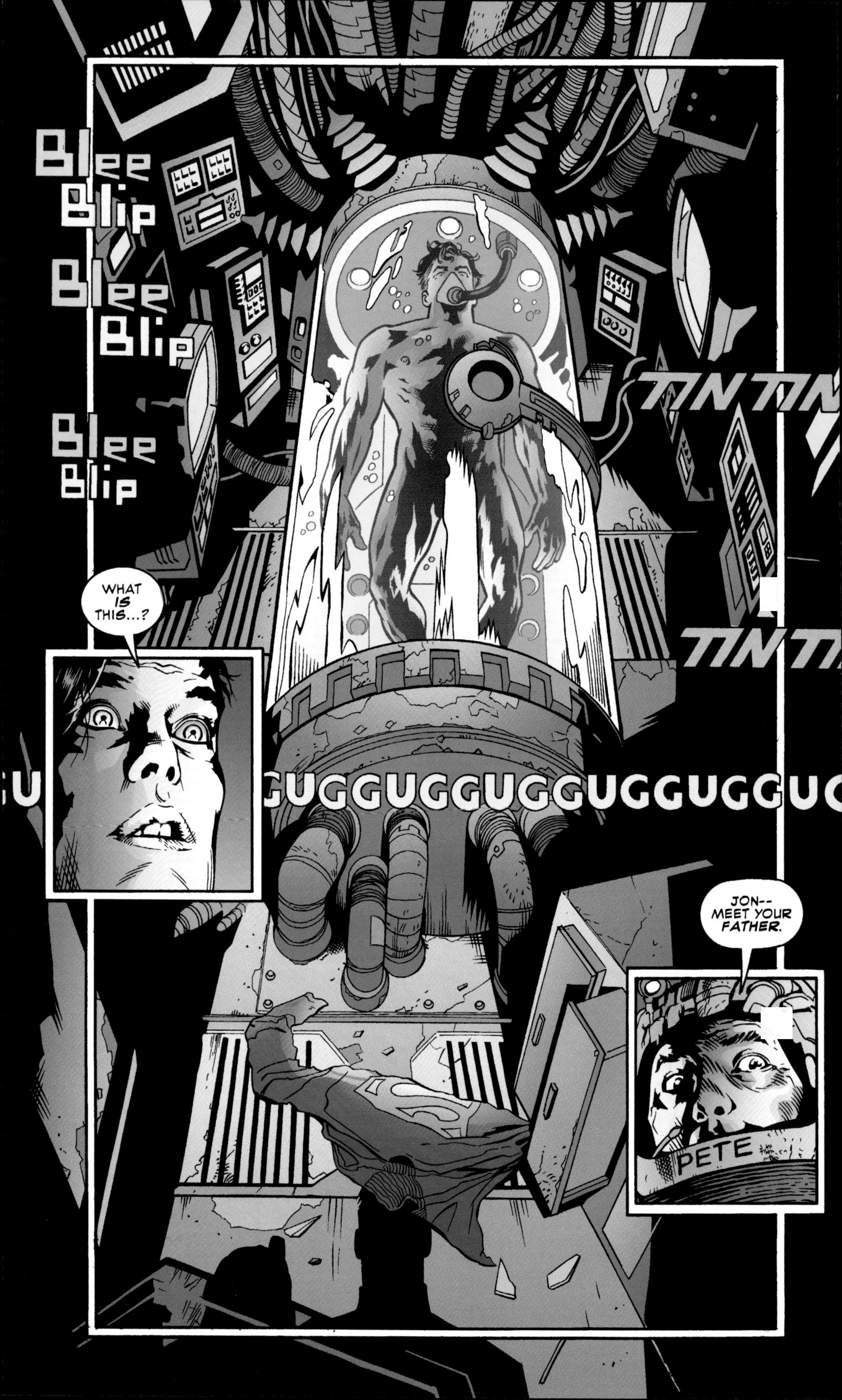
Blee
Blip
Blee
Blip
Blee
Blip
TINTIN
TINTIN
WHAT IS THIS...?
GUGGUGGUGGUGGUGGUG
JON-- MEET YOUR FATHER.
PETE

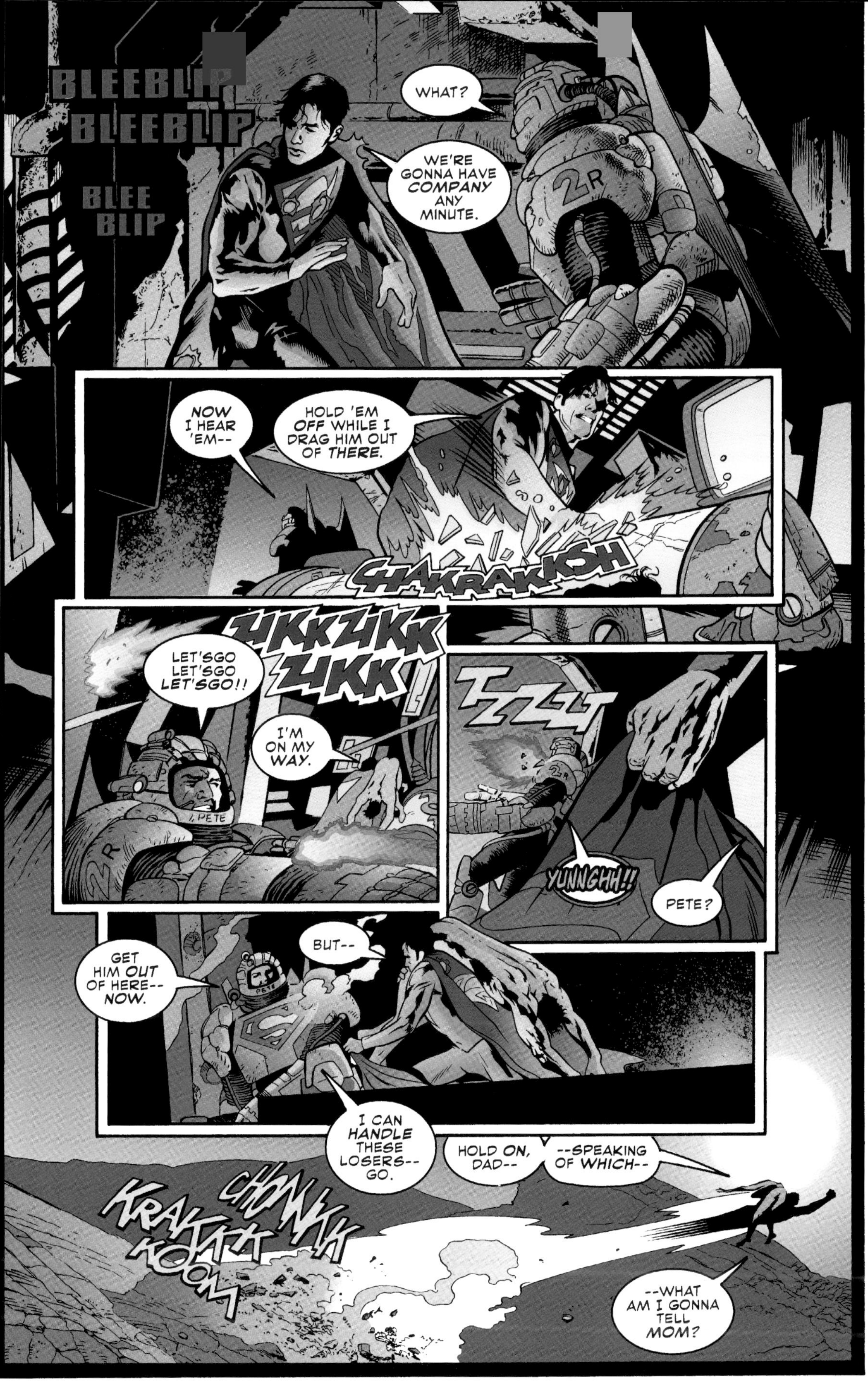
BLEEBLIP
BLEEBLIP
BLEE
BLIP
WHAT?
WE'RE GONNA HAVE COMPANY ANY MINUTE.
NOW I HEAR 'EM--
HOLD 'EM OFF WHILE I DRAG HIM OUT OF THERE.
CHAKRAKKISH
ZUKKZUKK ZUKK
LET'SGO LET'SGO LET'SGO!!
I'M ON MY WAY.
TZZZT
YUNNGHH!!
PETE?
PETE
GET HIM OUT OF HERE-- NOW.
BUT--
I CAN HANDLE THESE LOSERS-- GO.
HOLD ON, DAD--
--SPEAKING OF WHICH--
KRAKTAKK
CHOWKK
KOOM
--WHAT AM I GONNA TELL MOM?

SHE'S HOME...

...THEY'RE STILL INSIDE.

The BOMBS

BEVERLY HILLS HIGH

NO CALLS

I FEEL SO WEAK.

FIFTEEN YEARS IN SOLITARY CONFINEMENT--

--AND WET, TOO--

--WEAK IS THE WORD.

BOMBS

BEVERLY HILLS

WHERE AM I?

AND WHO ARE YOU?

GIVE THESE A SHOT--

--I DON'T NEED THEM ANYMORE.

JON--

--GET YOUR DOWN HERE--AND RIGHT NOW.

I HEARD FROM SCHOOL.

I HAD TO LIE AND SAY YOU WERE SICK.

I HATE LYING-- ESPECIALLY FOR YOU.

WHO'S THAT?

MY MOM.

WHERE AM I?

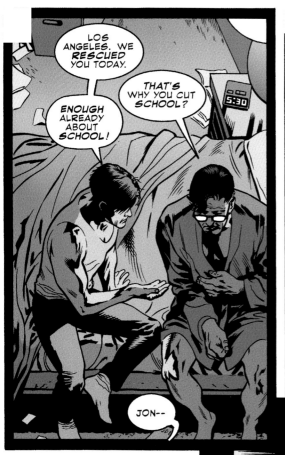

LOS ANGELES. WE *RESCUED* YOU TODAY.

THAT'S WHY YOU CUT SCHOOL?

ENOUGH ALREADY ABOUT *SCHOOL!*

JON--

I WAS IN *EUROPE.* THERE WAS A CIVIL WAR. ETHNIC CLEANSING--

--A *NICE* WAY TO SAY GENOCIDE.

THEY TOLD ME *NOT* TO GO, BUT I *HAD* TO...

DAMN IT, JON--

--I'M *TALKING* TO--

OH MY GOD.

LOIS.

CLARK.

NICE TO SEE YOU TWO CAN *STILL* FIND SOMETHING TO *SAY* AFTER ALL THESE YEARS.

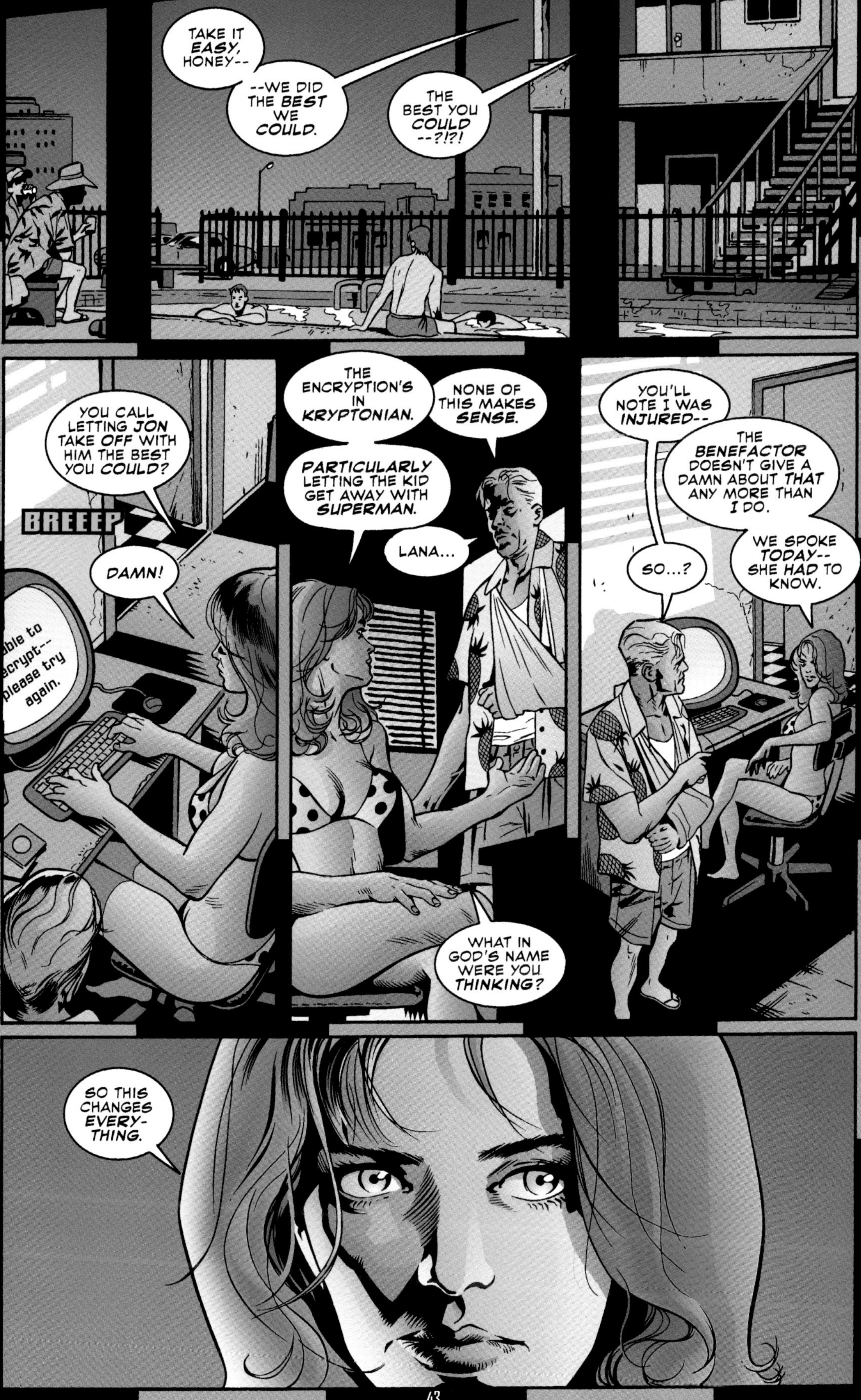
TAKE IT EASY, HONEY--
--WE DID THE BEST WE COULD.
THE BEST YOU COULD --?!?!
YOU CALL LETTING JON TAKE OFF WITH HIM THE BEST YOU COULD?
BREEEP
DAMN!
...able to ...ecrypt-- ...please try again.
THE ENCRYPTION'S IN KRYPTONIAN.
NONE OF THIS MAKES SENSE.
PARTICULARLY LETTING THE KID GET AWAY WITH SUPERMAN.
LANA...
WHAT IN GOD'S NAME WERE YOU THINKING?
YOU'LL NOTE I WAS INJURED--
THE BENEFACTOR DOESN'T GIVE A DAMN ABOUT THAT ANY MORE THAN I DO.
SO...?
WE SPOKE TODAY-- SHE HAD TO KNOW.
SO THIS CHANGES EVERY-THING.

PAMELA ACKROYD-- GBS ACTION NEWS WITH THIS *SPECIAL* REPORT ON THE *SUPERMEN'S* ON-GOING *REIGN* OF *TERROR.*

PAMELA ACKROYD

REPORTS ARE JUST COMING IN ON THE TERRORISTS' *ATTACK* AT A MEDICAL RESEARCH FACILITY IN *ATLANTA.*

OFFICIALS OF THE *C.D.C.* SAID THE SUPERMEN MADE OFF WITH AMPULES OF THE ANTHRAX AND EBOLA *VIRUSES.*

THE SUPERMEN LEFT NO *SURVIVORS.*

THIS REPORTER *DEPLORES* THESE SENSELESS ACTS OF *VIOLENCE.*

WE AT GBS *PLEAD* WITH THE JUSTICE LEAGUE OF AMERICA TO *STOP* THE SUPERMEN--BEFORE IT'S TOO *LATE* FOR ALL OF US.

PAMELA ACKROYD

PAMELA *ACKROYD--* GBS *ACTION* NEWS.

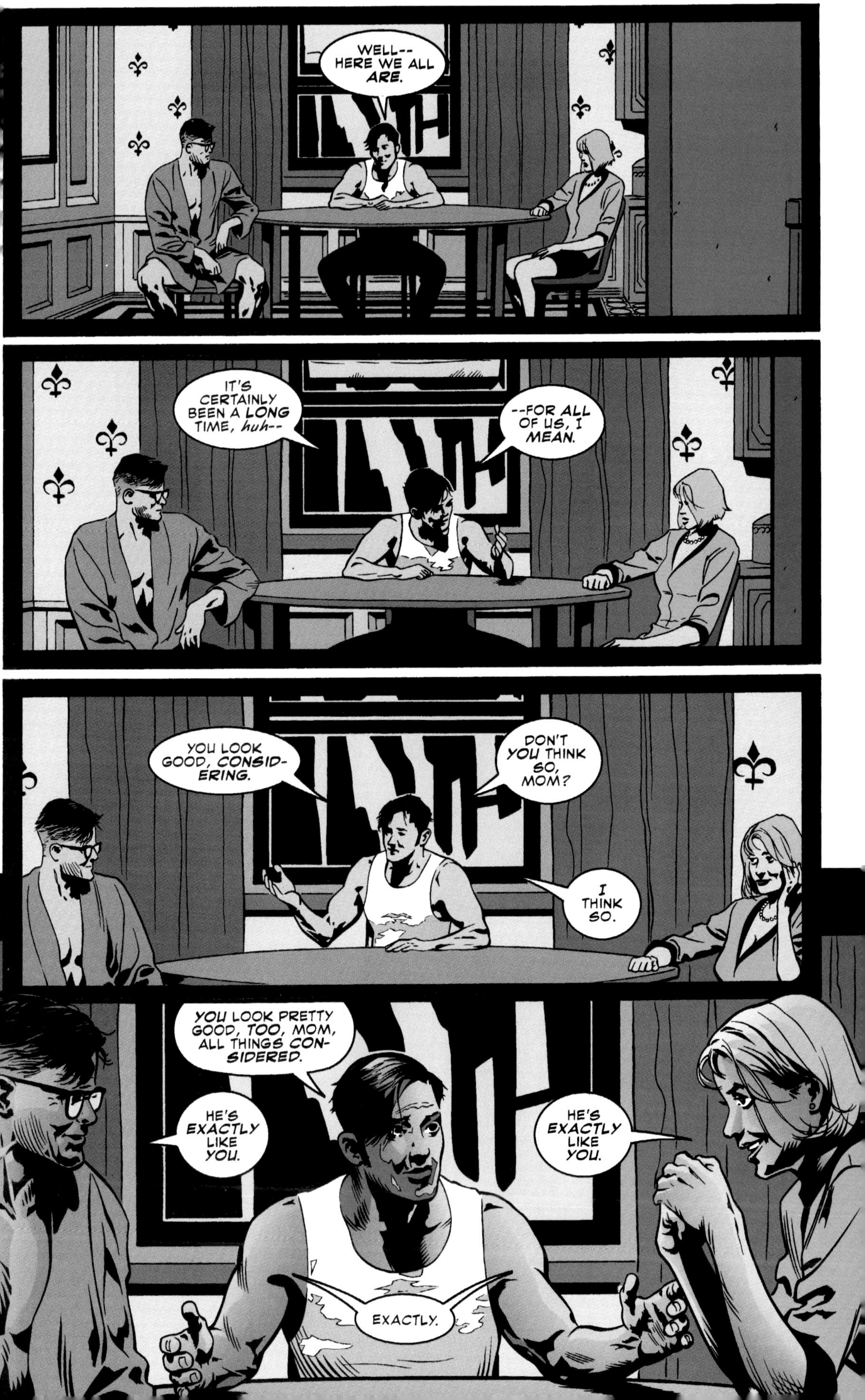
WELL--
HERE WE ALL
ARE.
IT'S
CERTAINLY
BEEN A LONG
TIME, huh--
--FOR ALL
OF US, I
MEAN.
YOU LOOK
GOOD, CONSID-
ERING.
DON'T
YOU THINK
SO,
MOM?
I
THINK
SO.
YOU LOOK PRETTY
GOOD, TOO, MOM,
ALL THINGS CON-
SIDERED.
HE'S
EXACTLY
LIKE
YOU.
HE'S
EXACTLY
LIKE
YOU.
EXACTLY.

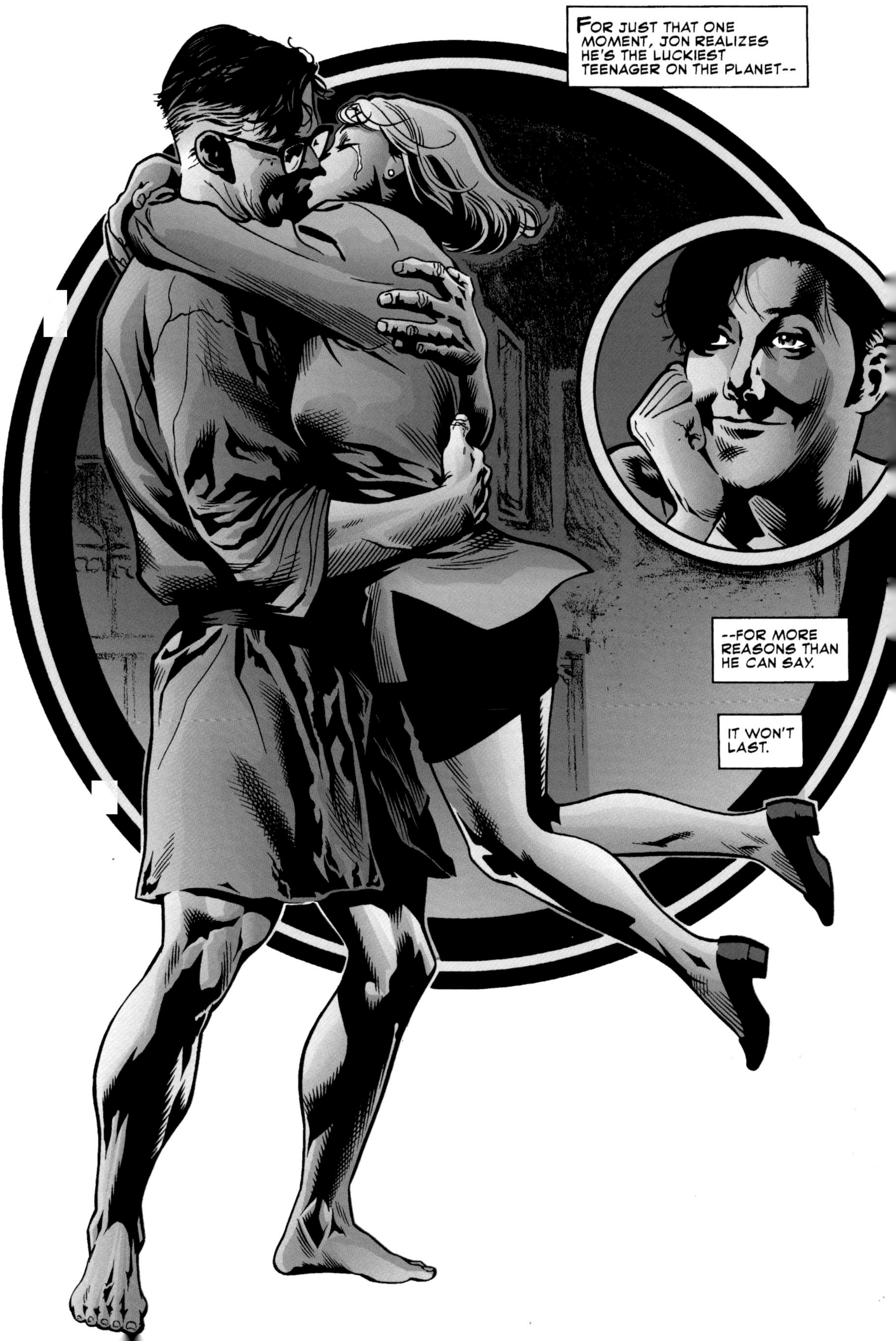
FOR JUST THAT ONE MOMENT, JON REALIZES HE'S THE LUCKIEST TEENAGER ON THE PLANET--
--FOR MORE REASONS THAN HE CAN SAY.
IT WON'T LAST.

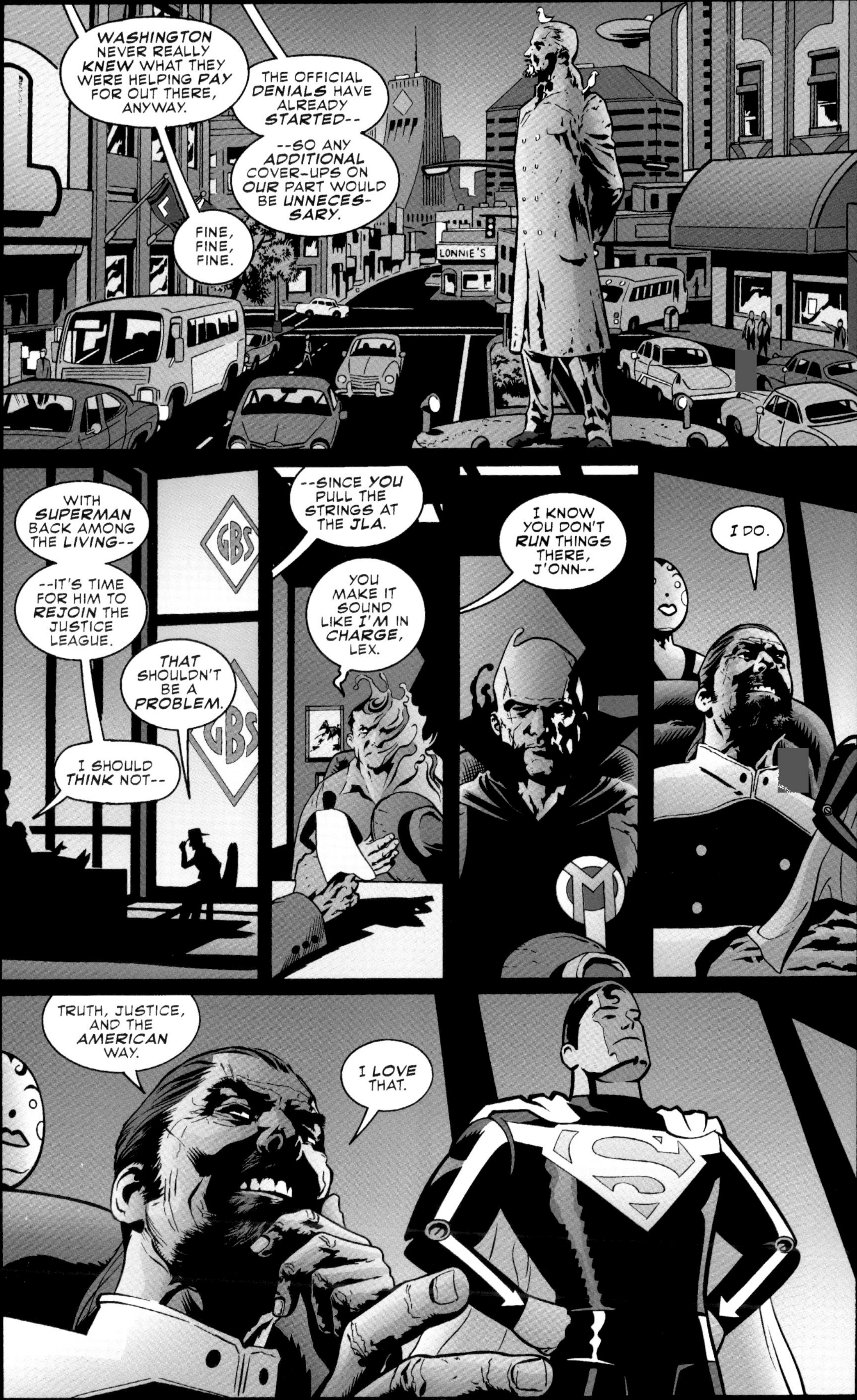
WASHINGTON NEVER REALLY KNEW WHAT THEY WERE HELPING PAY FOR OUT THERE, ANYWAY.
THE OFFICIAL DENIALS HAVE ALREADY STARTED--
--SO ANY ADDITIONAL COVER-UPS ON OUR PART WOULD BE UNNECES-SARY.
FINE, FINE, FINE.
LONNIE'S
WITH SUPERMAN BACK AMONG THE LIVING--
--IT'S TIME FOR HIM TO REJOIN THE JUSTICE LEAGUE.
THAT SHOULDN'T BE A PROBLEM.
I SHOULD THINK NOT--
--SINCE YOU PULL THE STRINGS AT THE JLA.
YOU MAKE IT SOUND LIKE I'M IN CHARGE, LEX.
I KNOW YOU DON'T RUN THINGS THERE, J'ONN--
I DO.
TRUTH, JUSTICE, AND THE AMERICAN WAY.
I LOVE THAT.

CAN'T DO IT SATURDAY--

--MY KID'S GOT SOCCER.

MONDAY?

MAYBE...

I'M JUST SAYING YOU SHOULD THINK ABOUT IT--

--ATLANTIS TURNS OVER MORE IN TOURISM THAN WE EVER DID ON KELP PRODUCTION.

I UNDERSTAND-- BUT AMAZONIUM WAS A GIFT FROM THE GODS TO MY MOTHER--

--A PUBLIC OFFERING MAKES ME A LITTLE QUEASY.

INCOMING CALL-- 3105556701.

LOIS?

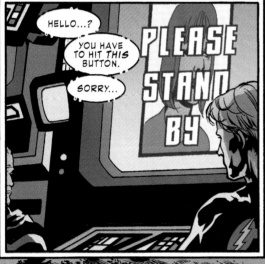

HELLO...?

YOU HAVE TO HIT THIS BUTTON.

SORRY...

PLEASE STAND BY

I'M STILL GETTING USED TO THE TECH- NOLOGY.

SO--

--I GUESS YOU'RE WONDERING WHERE I'VE BEEN ALL THESE YEARS.

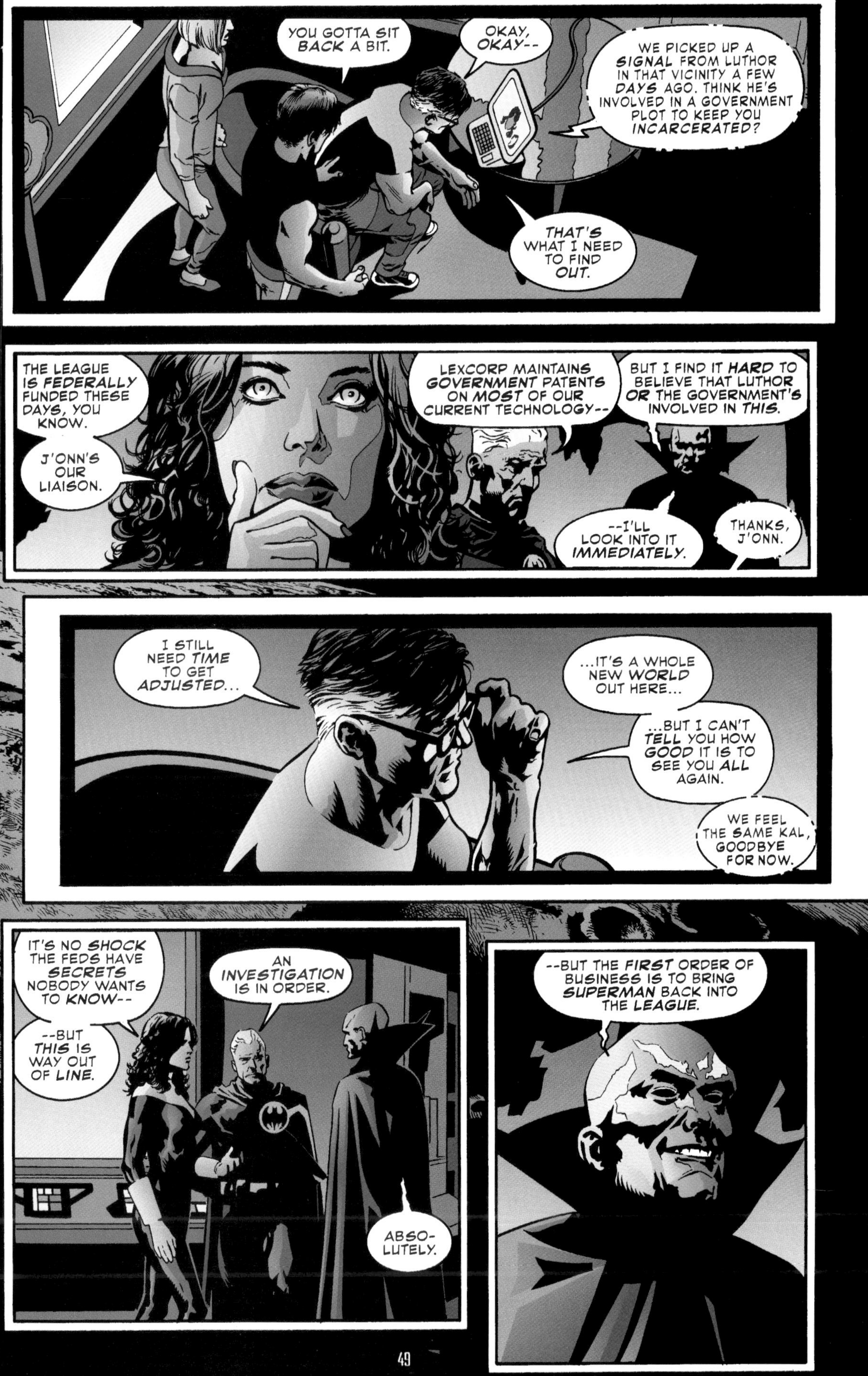
YOU GOTTA SIT BACK A BIT.
OKAY, OKAY--
WE PICKED UP A SIGNAL FROM LUTHOR IN THAT VICINITY A FEW DAYS AGO. THINK HE'S INVOLVED IN A GOVERNMENT PLOT TO KEEP YOU INCARCERATED?
THAT'S WHAT I NEED TO FIND OUT.
THE LEAGUE IS FEDERALLY FUNDED THESE DAYS, YOU KNOW.
J'ONN'S OUR LIAISON.
LEXCORP MAINTAINS GOVERNMENT PATENTS ON MOST OF OUR CURRENT TECHNOLOGY--
BUT I FIND IT HARD TO BELIEVE THAT LUTHOR OR THE GOVERNMENT'S INVOLVED IN THIS.
--I'LL LOOK INTO IT IMMEDIATELY.
THANKS, J'ONN.
I STILL NEED TIME TO GET ADJUSTED...
...IT'S A WHOLE NEW WORLD OUT HERE...
...BUT I CAN'T TELL YOU HOW GOOD IT IS TO SEE YOU ALL AGAIN.
WE FEEL THE SAME KAL, GOODBYE FOR NOW.
IT'S NO SHOCK THE FEDS HAVE SECRETS NOBODY WANTS TO KNOW--
--BUT THIS IS WAY OUT OF LINE.
AN INVESTIGATION IS IN ORDER.
ABSO-LUTELY.
--BUT THE FIRST ORDER OF BUSINESS IS TO BRING SUPERMAN BACK INTO THE LEAGUE.

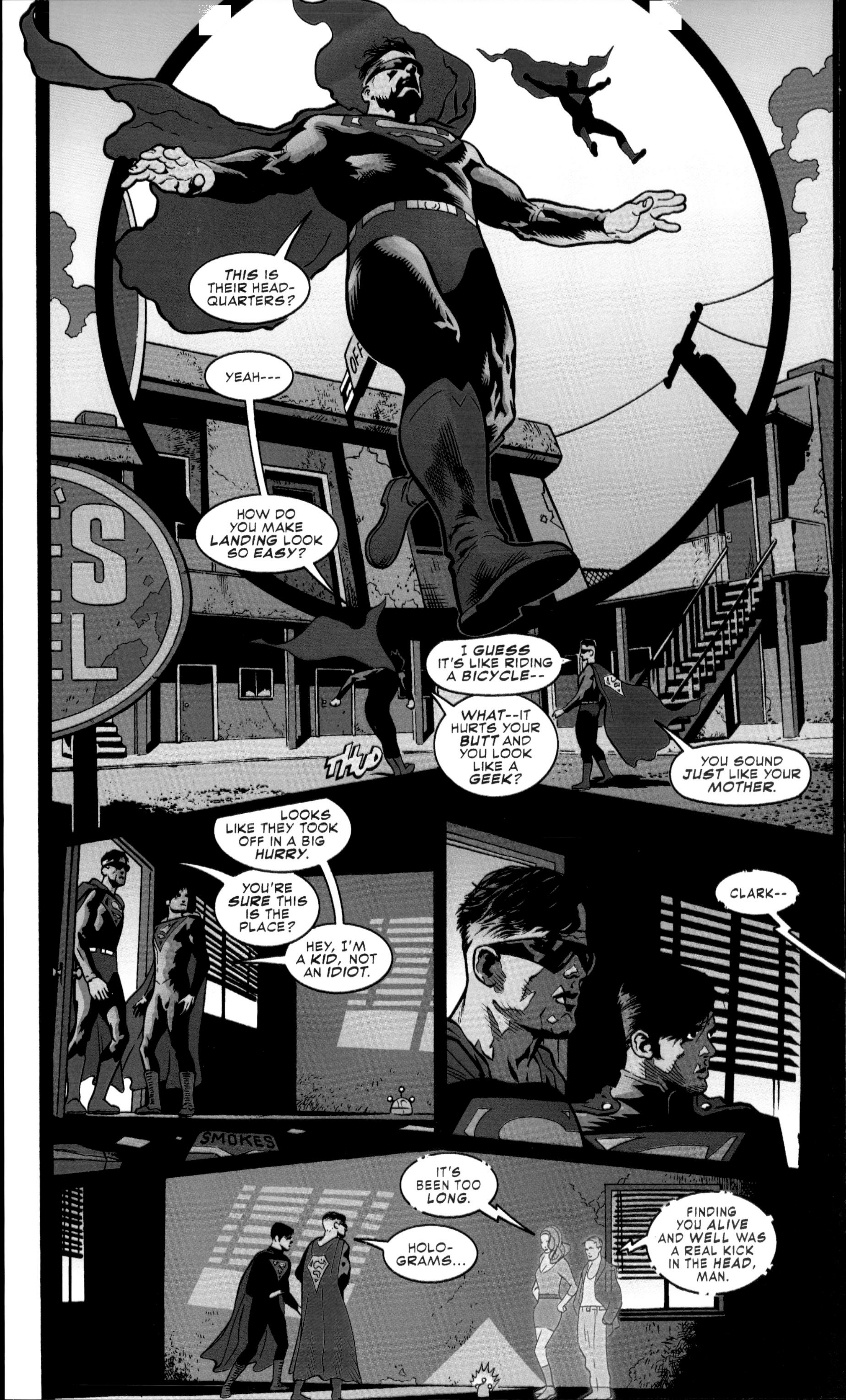
THIS IS THEIR HEAD-QUARTERS?
YEAH---
HOW DO YOU MAKE LANDING LOOK SO EASY?
I GUESS IT'S LIKE RIDING A BICYCLE--
WHAT--IT HURTS YOUR BUTT AND YOU LOOK LIKE A GEEK?
YOU SOUND JUST LIKE YOUR MOTHER.
THUD
LOOKS LIKE THEY TOOK OFF IN A BIG HURRY.
YOU'RE SURE THIS IS THE PLACE?
HEY, I'M A KID, NOT AN IDIOT.
CLARK--
SMOKES
IT'S BEEN TOO LONG.
HOLO-GRAMS...
FINDING YOU ALIVE AND WELL WAS A REAL KICK IN THE HEAD, MAN.

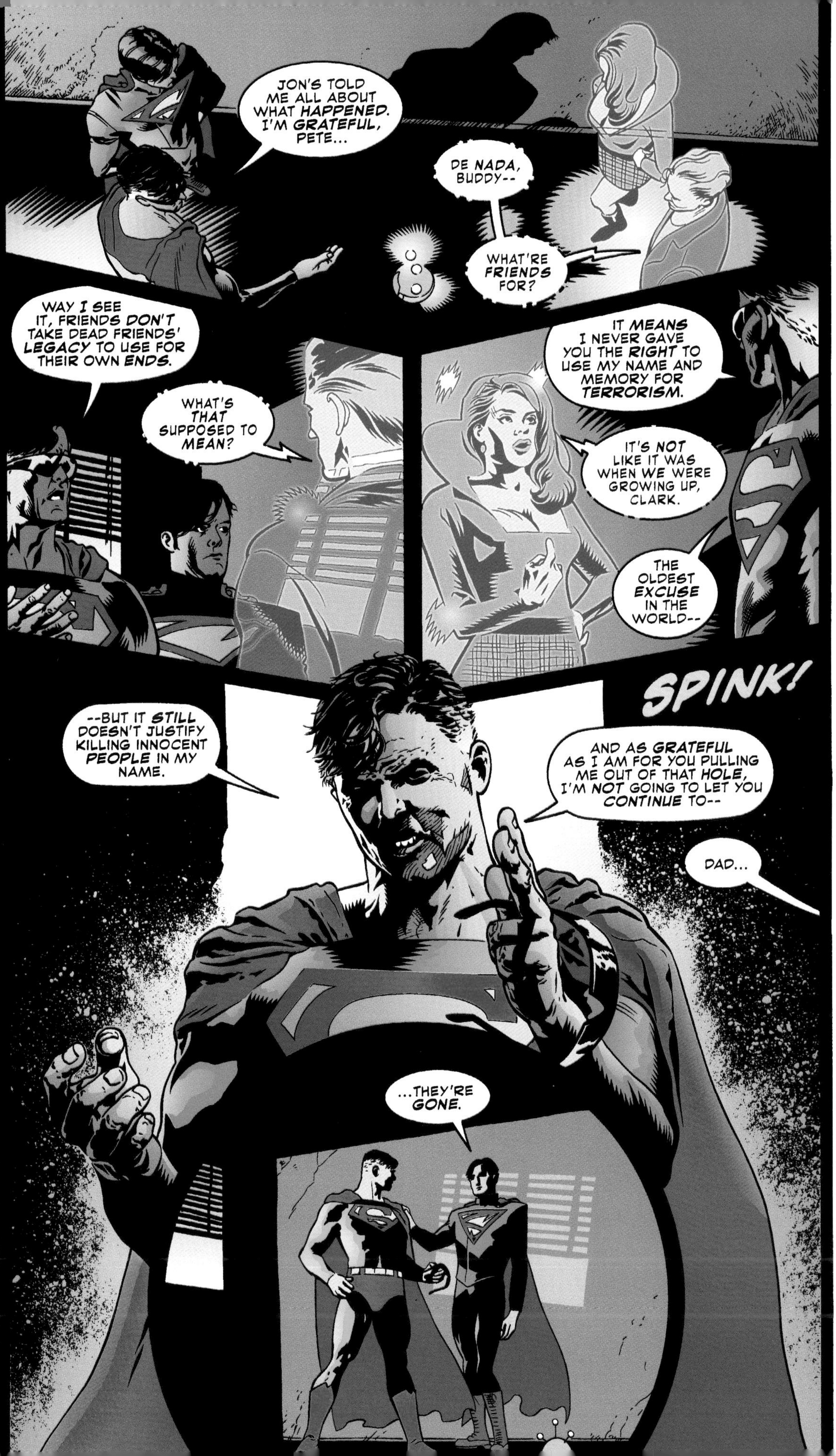

JON'S TOLD ME ALL ABOUT WHAT HAPPENED. I'M GRATEFUL, PETE...
DE NADA, BUDDY--
WHAT'RE FRIENDS FOR?
WAY I SEE IT, FRIENDS DON'T TAKE DEAD FRIENDS' LEGACY TO USE FOR THEIR OWN ENDS.
WHAT'S THAT SUPPOSED TO MEAN?
IT MEANS I NEVER GAVE YOU THE RIGHT TO USE MY NAME AND MEMORY FOR TERRORISM.
IT'S NOT LIKE IT WAS WHEN WE WERE GROWING UP, CLARK.
THE OLDEST EXCUSE IN THE WORLD--
SPINK!
--BUT IT STILL DOESN'T JUSTIFY KILLING INNOCENT PEOPLE IN MY NAME.
AND AS GRATEFUL AS I AM FOR YOU PULLING ME OUT OF THAT HOLE, I'M NOT GOING TO LET YOU CONTINUE TO--
DAD...
...THEY'RE GONE.

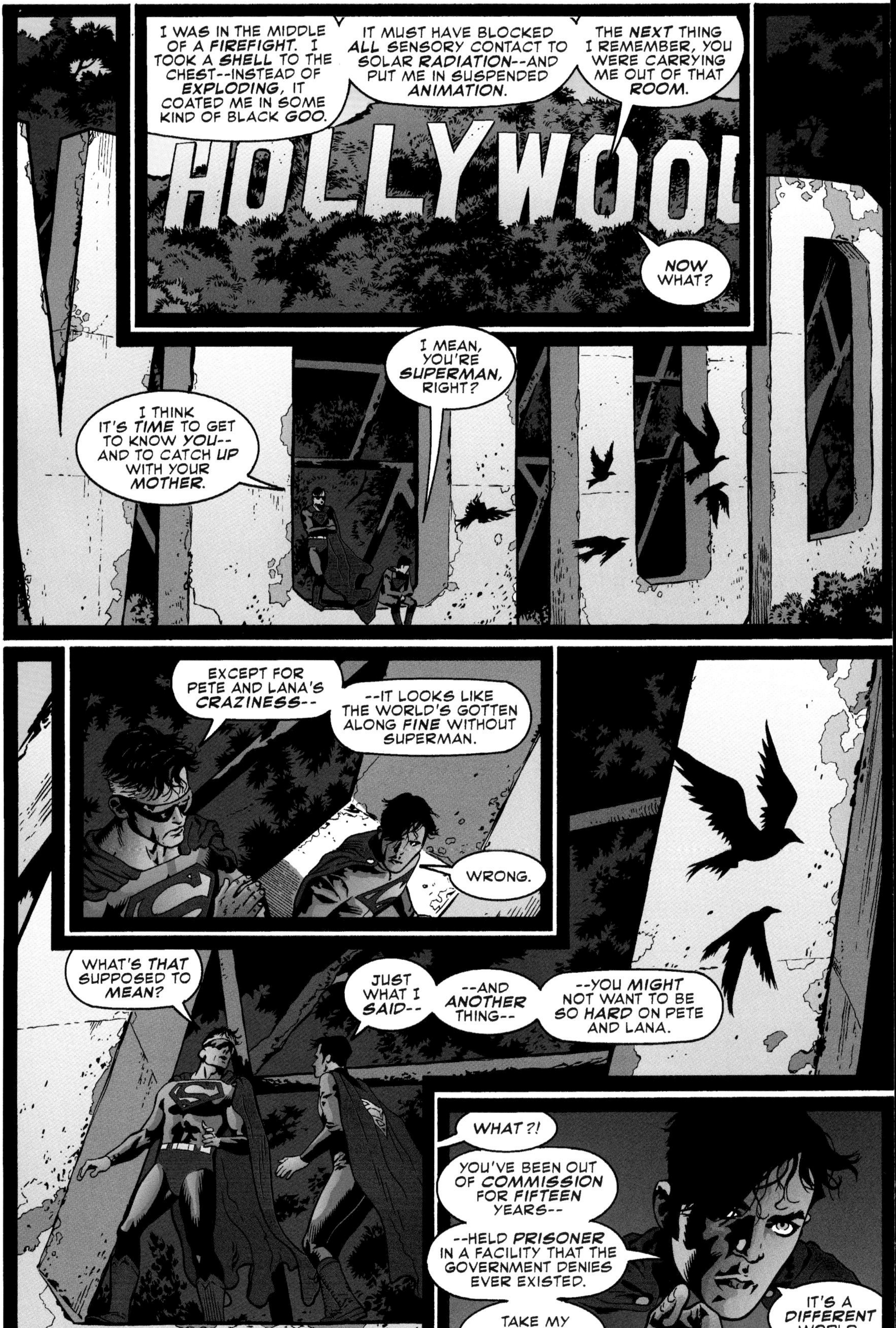
I WAS IN THE MIDDLE OF A FIREFIGHT. I TOOK A SHELL TO THE CHEST--INSTEAD OF EXPLODING, IT COATED ME IN SOME KIND OF BLACK GOO.
IT MUST HAVE BLOCKED ALL SENSORY CONTACT TO SOLAR RADIATION--AND PUT ME IN SUSPENDED ANIMATION.
THE NEXT THING I REMEMBER, YOU WERE CARRYING ME OUT OF THAT ROOM.
HOLLYWOO
NOW WHAT?
I MEAN, YOU'RE SUPERMAN, RIGHT?
I THINK IT'S TIME TO GET TO KNOW YOU--AND TO CATCH UP WITH YOUR MOTHER.
EXCEPT FOR PETE AND LANA'S CRAZINESS--
--IT LOOKS LIKE THE WORLD'S GOTTEN ALONG FINE WITHOUT SUPERMAN.
WRONG.
WHAT'S THAT SUPPOSED TO MEAN?
JUST WHAT I SAID--
--AND ANOTHER THING--
--YOU MIGHT NOT WANT TO BE SO HARD ON PETE AND LANA.
WHAT?!
YOU'VE BEEN OUT OF COMMISSION FOR FIFTEEN YEARS--
--HELD PRISONER IN A FACILITY THAT THE GOVERNMENT DENIES EVER EXISTED.
TAKE MY WORD FOR IT--
IT'S A DIFFERENT WORLD.

53

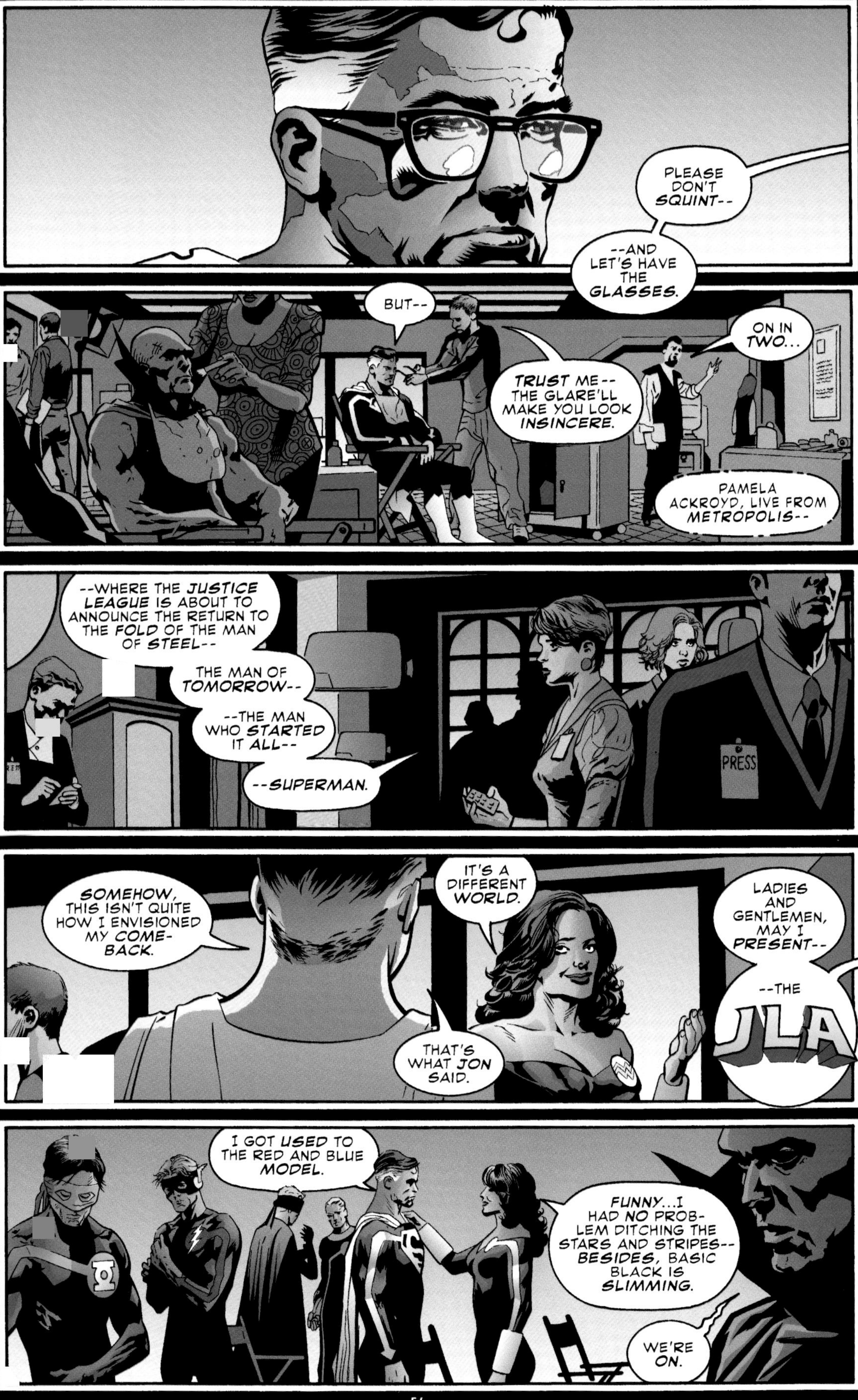

PLEASE DON'T SQUINT--
--AND LET'S HAVE THE GLASSES.
BUT--
TRUST ME--THE GLARE'LL MAKE YOU LOOK INSINCERE.
ON IN TWO...
PAMELA ACKROYD, LIVE FROM METROPOLIS--
--WHERE THE JUSTICE LEAGUE IS ABOUT TO ANNOUNCE THE RETURN TO THE FOLD OF THE MAN OF STEEL--
THE MAN OF TOMORROW--
--THE MAN WHO STARTED IT ALL--
--SUPERMAN.
PRESS
SOMEHOW, THIS ISN'T QUITE HOW I ENVISIONED MY COME-BACK.
IT'S A DIFFERENT WORLD.
THAT'S WHAT JON SAID.
LADIES AND GENTLEMEN, MAY I PRESENT--
--THE JLA
I GOT USED TO THE RED AND BLUE MODEL.
FUNNY...I HAD NO PROB-LEM DITCHING THE STARS AND STRIPES--BESIDES, BASIC BLACK IS SLIMMING.
WE'RE ON.

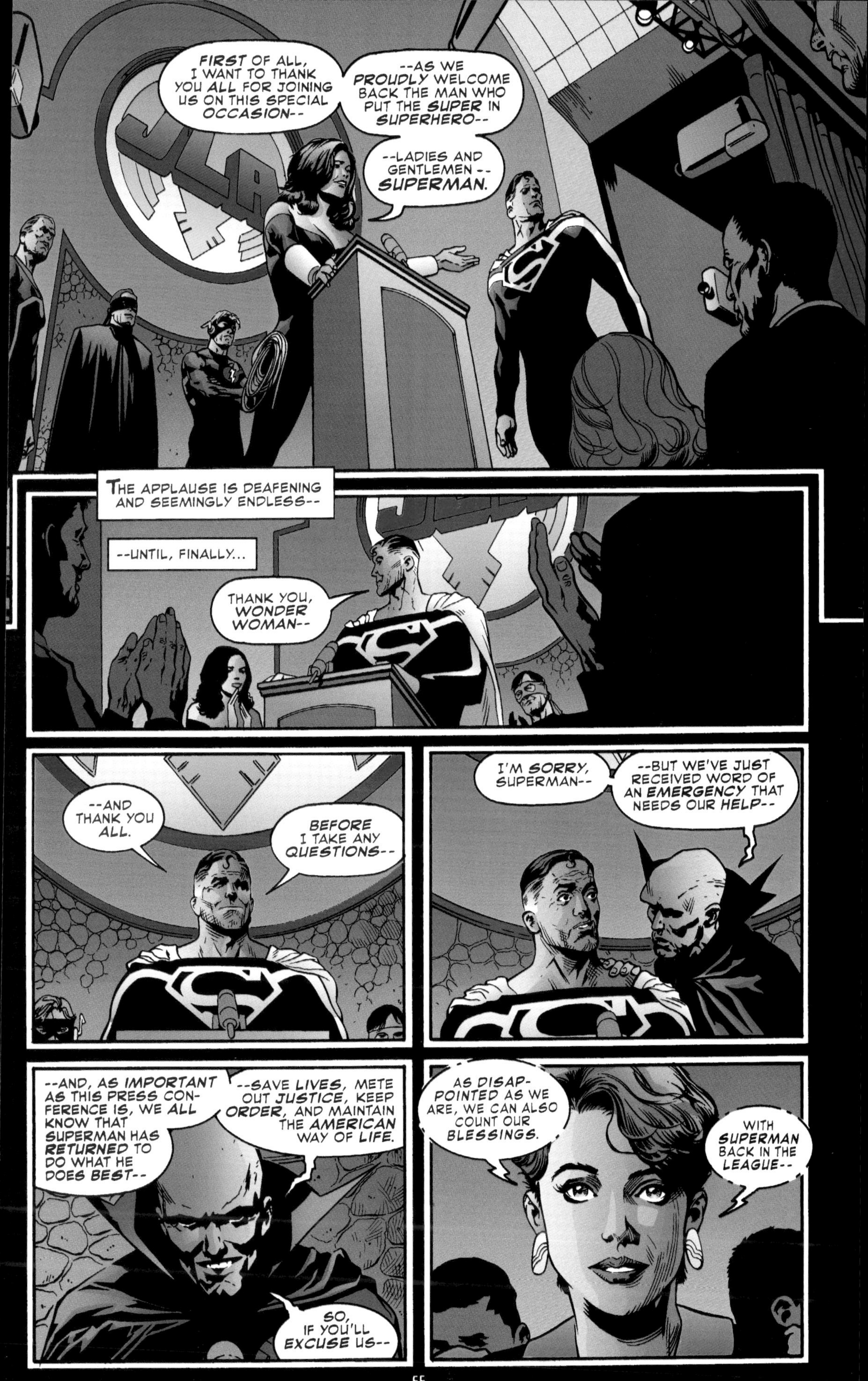
FIRST OF ALL, I WANT TO THANK YOU ALL FOR JOINING US ON THIS SPECIAL OCCASION--
--AS WE PROUDLY WELCOME BACK THE MAN WHO PUT THE SUPER IN SUPERHERO--
--LADIES AND GENTLEMEN -- SUPERMAN.
THE APPLAUSE IS DEAFENING AND SEEMINGLY ENDLESS--
--UNTIL, FINALLY...
THANK YOU, WONDER WOMAN--
--AND THANK YOU ALL.
BEFORE I TAKE ANY QUESTIONS--
I'M SORRY, SUPERMAN--
--BUT WE'VE JUST RECEIVED WORD OF AN EMERGENCY THAT NEEDS OUR HELP--
--AND, AS IMPORTANT AS THIS PRESS CONFERENCE IS, WE ALL KNOW THAT SUPERMAN HAS RETURNED TO DO WHAT HE DOES BEST--
--SAVE LIVES, METE OUT JUSTICE, KEEP ORDER, AND MAINTAIN THE AMERICAN WAY OF LIFE.
SO, IF YOU'LL EXCUSE US--
AS DISAPPOINTED AS WE ARE, WE CAN ALSO COUNT OUR BLESSINGS.
WITH SUPERMAN BACK IN THE LEAGUE--

BRINGS YOU *BACK,* HUH?

I COULDN'T *WAIT* TO GET *OUT.*

IT WAS STIFLING, PETTY AND VENAL--WITH EVERYBODY KNOWING *EVERYBODY* ELSE'S *BUSINESS* ALL THE TIME.

BUT *THANKS* TO THAT SMALL-MINDEDNESS, WE KNEW EVERY-BODY'S BUSINESS, TOO--

I WANNA *FIND* IT AND GET THE HELL *OUT* OF HERE.

GOT IT--

--RIGHT WHERE THE KENTS' *BARN* USED TO BE.

--SO IF IT'S STILL *HERE,* WE'LL *FIND* IT.

YOU'RE STANDING ON *TOP* OF IT.

LET'S LOOK.

IT'S *HERE,* LANA--

--GOD-- IT'S SO TINY.

GRAB IT AND LET'S GET GONE--

--THE *SHERIFF'S* GONNA BE SWINGING BY IN ABOUT 90 SECONDS.

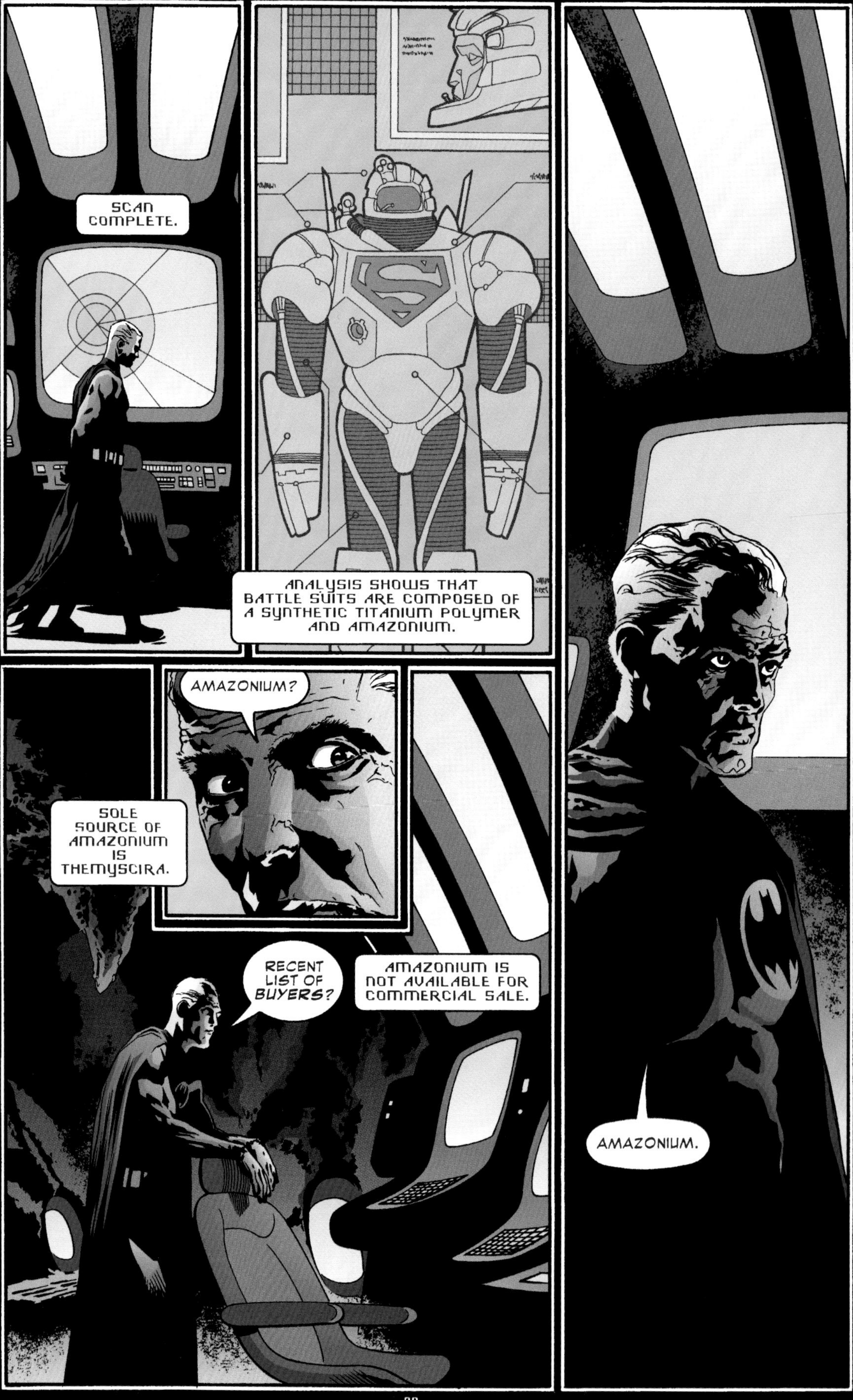
SCAN COMPLETE.
ANALYSIS SHOWS THAT BATTLE SUITS ARE COMPOSED OF A SYNTHETIC TITANIUM POLYMER AND AMAZONIUM.
AMAZONIUM?
SOLE SOURCE OF AMAZONIUM IS THEMYSCIRA.
RECENT LIST OF BUYERS?
AMAZONIUM IS NOT AVAILABLE FOR COMMERCIAL SALE.
AMAZONIUM.

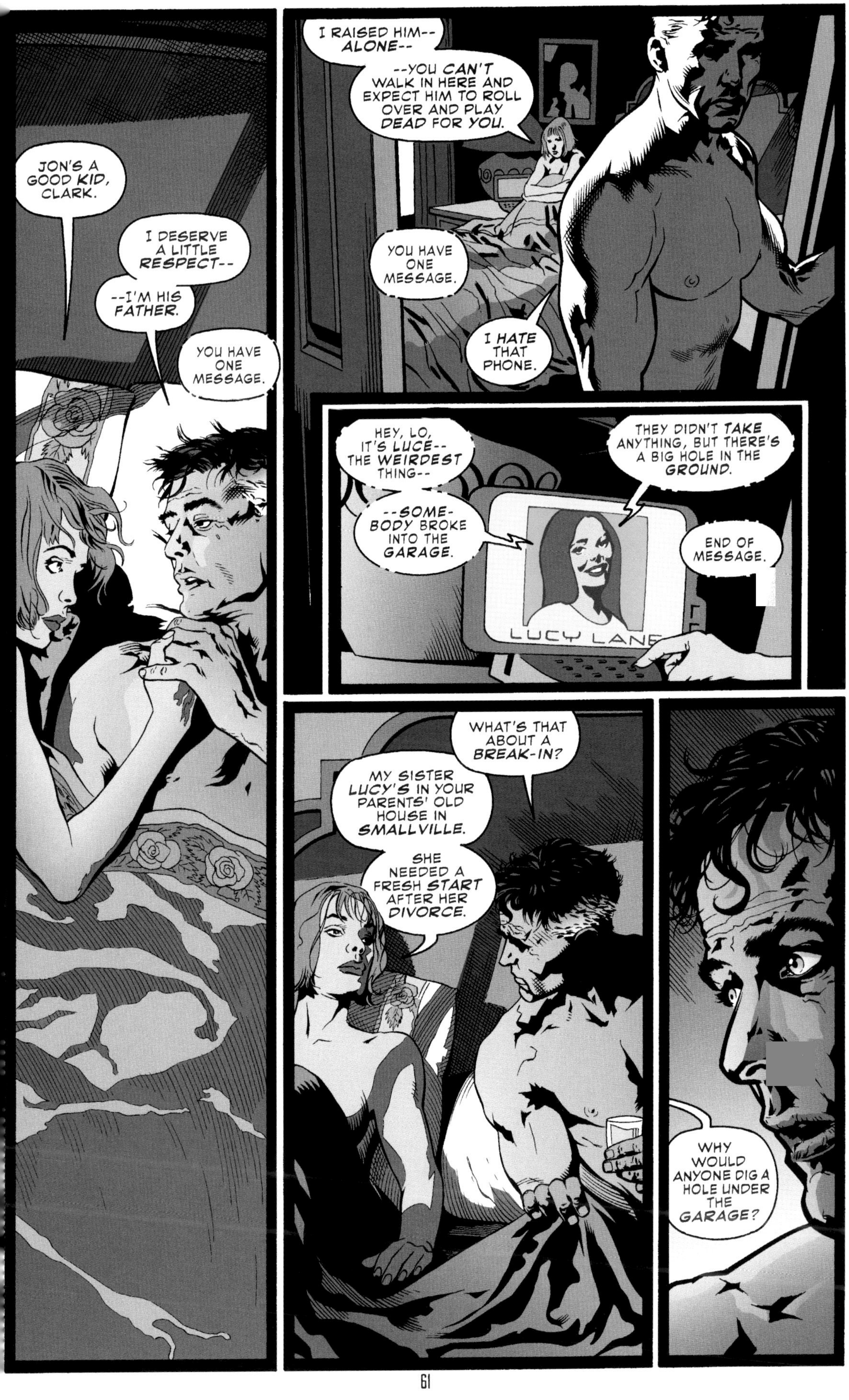
JON'S A GOOD KID, CLARK.
I DESERVE A LITTLE RESPECT--
--I'M HIS FATHER.
YOU HAVE ONE MESSAGE.
I RAISED HIM-- ALONE--
--YOU CAN'T WALK IN HERE AND EXPECT HIM TO ROLL OVER AND PLAY DEAD FOR YOU.
YOU HAVE ONE MESSAGE.
I HATE THAT PHONE.
HEY, LO, IT'S LUCE-- THE WEIRDEST THING--
--SOME-BODY BROKE INTO THE GARAGE.
THEY DIDN'T TAKE ANYTHING, BUT THERE'S A BIG HOLE IN THE GROUND.
LUCY LANE
END OF MESSAGE.
WHAT'S THAT ABOUT A BREAK-IN?
MY SISTER LUCY'S IN YOUR PARENTS' OLD HOUSE IN SMALLVILLE.
SHE NEEDED A FRESH START AFTER HER DIVORCE.
WHY WOULD ANYONE DIG A HOLE UNDER THE GARAGE?

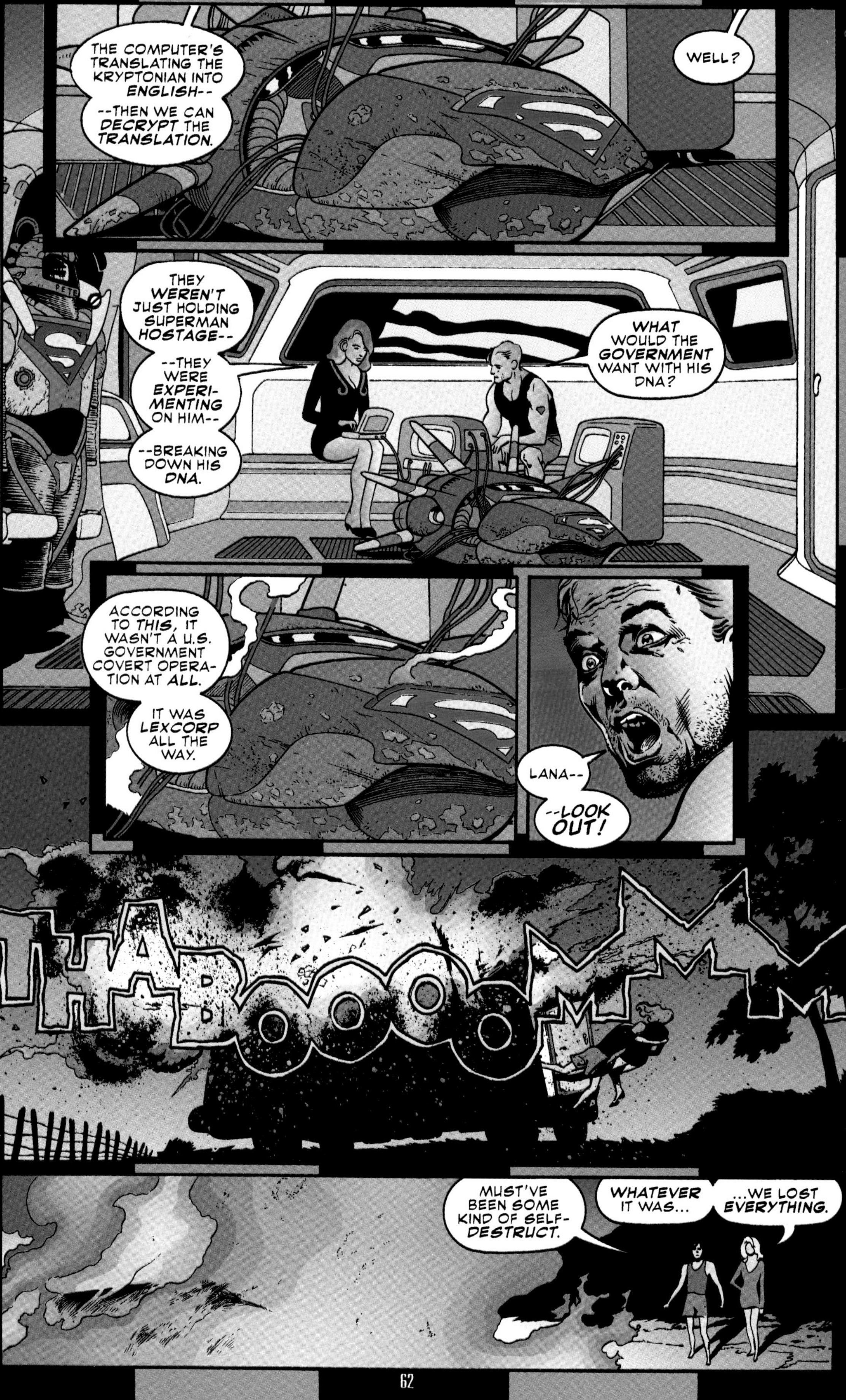
THE COMPUTER'S TRANSLATING THE KRYPTONIAN INTO ENGLISH--
--THEN WE CAN DECRYPT THE TRANSLATION.
WELL?
PETE
THEY WEREN'T JUST HOLDING SUPERMAN HOSTAGE--
--THEY WERE EXPERI-MENTING ON HIM--
--BREAKING DOWN HIS DNA.
WHAT WOULD THE GOVERNMENT WANT WITH HIS DNA?
ACCORDING TO THIS, IT WASN'T A U.S. GOVERNMENT COVERT OPERA-TION AT ALL.
IT WAS LEXCORP ALL THE WAY.
LANA--
--LOOK OUT!
THADBOOOOOMMMM
MUST'VE BEEN SOME KIND OF SELF-DESTRUCT.
WHATEVER IT WAS...
...WE LOST EVERYTHING.

SEVENTEEN YEARS AGO, I MADE A MOMENTOUS DISCOVERY...

...AND EACH OF YOU, IN YOUR OWN WAY, HELPED ME PROFIT FROM THAT DISCOVERY.

SOME HELPED WITH TECHNOLOGY--

--TRANSFORMING SOCIETY...ALLOWING IT TO PROSPER BEYOND OUR WILDEST IMAGINATION.

SOME MANUFACTURED THE DRUG "K" AND SPREAD IT ACROSS THE COUNTRY, RAVAGING OUR INNER CITIES--

--CREATING A CHAOTIC ENVIRONMENT YEARNING FOR LAW AND ORDER--

BY CLOSE OF BUSINESS FRIDAY, LEXCORP WILL HAVE BOUGHT UP SIXTY-ONE PERCENT OF AMERICA'S NATIONAL DEBT--

--PROVIDED BY PUBLIC SERVANTS WHO TOOK MY ADVICE AND MY MONEY.

AND FINALLY, THERE ARE THOSE WITH EVEN DEEPER SECRETS AND HIDDEN AGENDAS--

--ALL PART OF THE GRAND SCHEME OF THINGS.

--GIVING ME CONTROLLING INTEREST IN THE U.S. GOVERNMENT!

NOTHING...

IT WAS RIGHT HERE--I KNOW IT.

UNFORTU-NATELY, X-RAY VISION DIDN'T COME WITH THE *OPTIONS* PACKAGE--

--SO I HAVE TO DO IT THE *HARD* WAY.

I DON'T KNOW HOW THEY *DID* IT--

--BUT THERE'S *NOTHING* HERE.

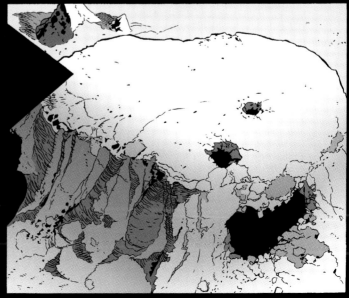

65

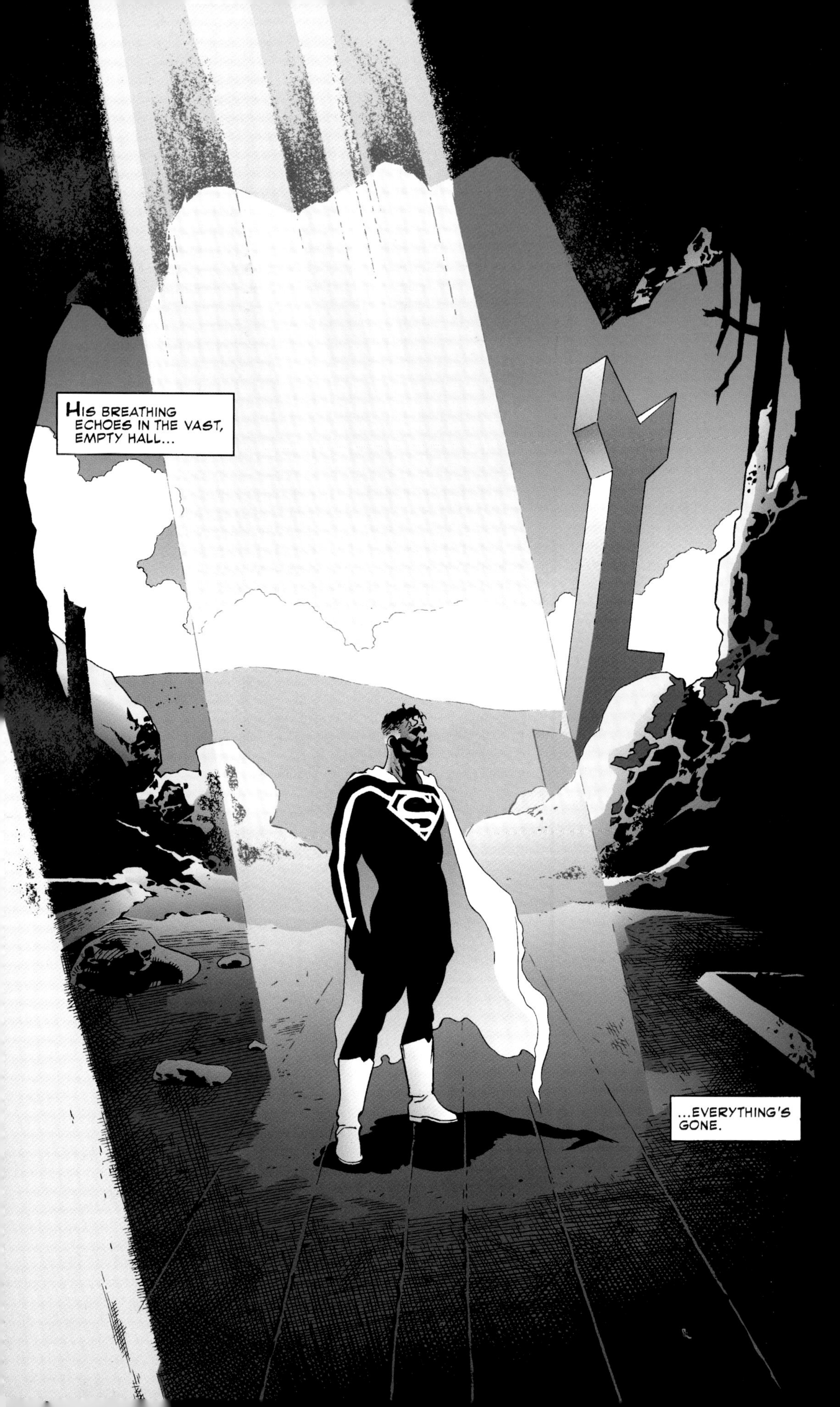
HIS BREATHING ECHOES IN THE VAST, EMPTY HALL...
...EVERYTHING'S GONE.

NOT *BAD* FOR AN *OLD BROAD,* HUH?

SO--WERE YOU PLANNING TO SIT THERE AND *WATCH* UNTIL I GOT *DRESSED*--

--OR WERE YOU GOING TO SNEAK *OUT* BEFORE I KNEW YOU WERE THERE ALL ALONG?

I *DIDN'T* WANT TO BRING IT *UP* WITH THE OTHERS PRESENT...

BUT I COMPLETED THE *ANALYSIS* OF THE *SUPERMEN'S BATTLE SUITS*--

THAT'S WHY YOU'RE PLAYING PEEPING TOM IN MY *BEDROOM*?

DIANA--

WHAT EXACTLY DO YOU *WANT,* BRUCE?

DIANA...

67

I ASKED YOU A QUESTION.

WSHAM

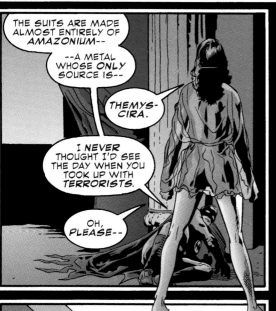

THE SUITS ARE MADE ALMOST ENTIRELY OF *AMAZONIUM*--

--A METAL WHOSE *ONLY* SOURCE IS--

THEMYS-CIRA.

I *NEVER* THOUGHT I'D SEE THE DAY WHEN YOU TOOK UP WITH *TERRORISTS.*

OH, *PLEASE*--

LET'S *FACE IT,* BRUCE, *YOU'RE* A MULTI-BILLIONAIRE.

AQUAMAN AND I ARE *ROYALTY,* J'ONN'S AN *ALIEN,* FLASH AND GREEN LANTERN COLLECT A *HEFTY* PAY-CHECK.

WE LOST *TOUCH* WITH THE PEOPLE WE'RE SUPPOSED TO SERVE *YEARS* AGO.

BUT--

WE *PROSPER* AT THEIR *EXPENSE.*

MY *MISSION* WHEN I CAME TO MAN'S WORLD WAS TO MAKE IT A *BETTER PLACE*--

--HOW I CHOOSE TO *FULFILL* THAT *MISSION* IS MY *BUSINESS.*

THAT'S MY *FINAL WORD* ON THE SUBJECT.

DON'T LET THE *DOOR* HIT YOU ON THE WAY *OUT.*

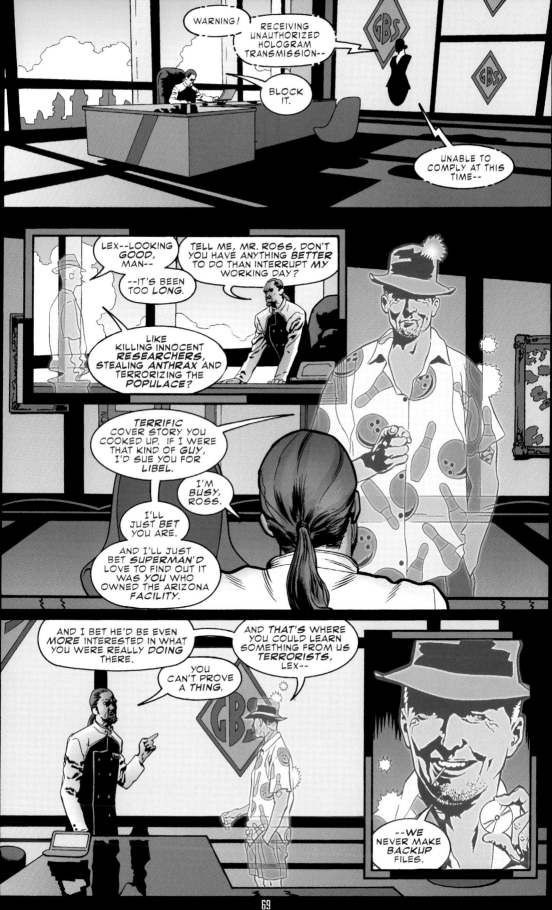

THIS HAS GONE ON LONG **ENOUGH.**

CLARK--JON IS YOUR SON--REGARDLESS OF HIS *POLITICS.*

JON, THIS IS YOUR *FATHER--* TREAT HIM **APPROPRIATELY.**

DO I MAKE MYSELF *CLEAR?*

ABSOLUTELY, LOIS.

CRYSTAL, MOM.

FINE. I'VE GOT A *SALON* APPOINTMENT--

IT'LL TAKE AN HOUR AND A HALF. YOU'VE GOT 'TIL I GET *BACK* TO START *BEHAVING* LIKE HUMAN BEINGS.

SHE *ALWAYS* BEEN LIKE THIS?

uh-huhn.

AND YOU *STILL* MARRIED HER?

CLARK KENT MARRIED LOIS LANE.

uh-huhn.

SLAM

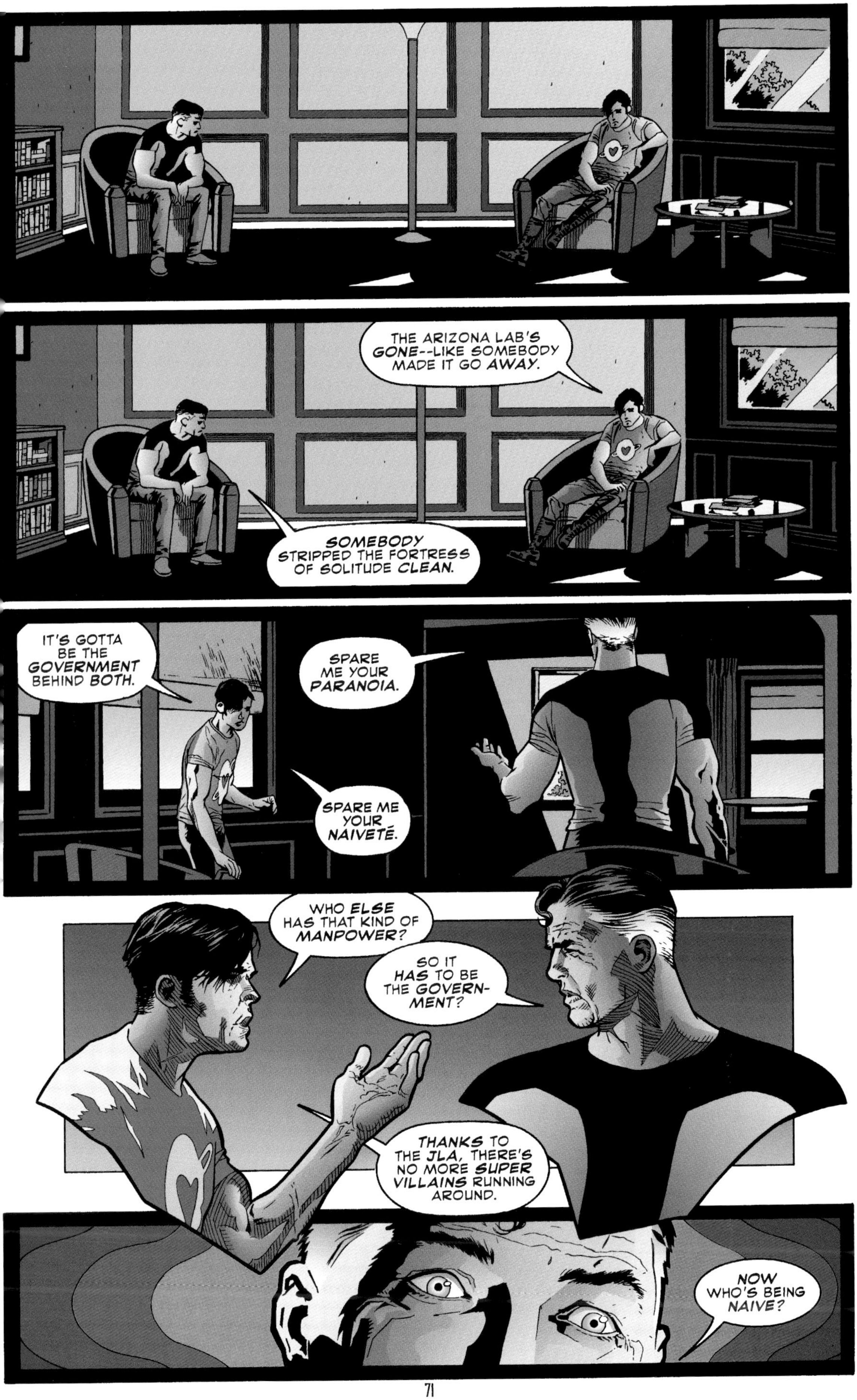
THE ARIZONA LAB'S GONE--LIKE SOMEBODY MADE IT GO AWAY.
SOMEBODY STRIPPED THE FORTRESS OF SOLITUDE CLEAN.
IT'S GOTTA BE THE GOVERNMENT BEHIND BOTH.
SPARE ME YOUR PARANOIA.
SPARE ME YOUR NAIVETÉ.
WHO ELSE HAS THAT KIND OF MANPOWER?
SO IT HAS TO BE THE GOVERN-MENT?
THANKS TO THE JLA, THERE'S NO MORE SUPER VILLAINS RUNNING AROUND.
NOW WHO'S BEING NAIVE?

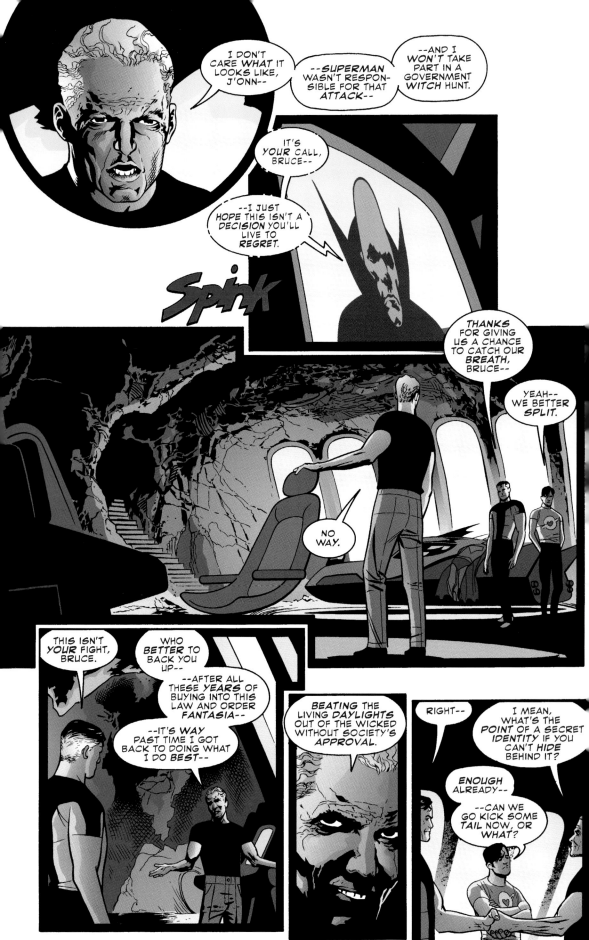

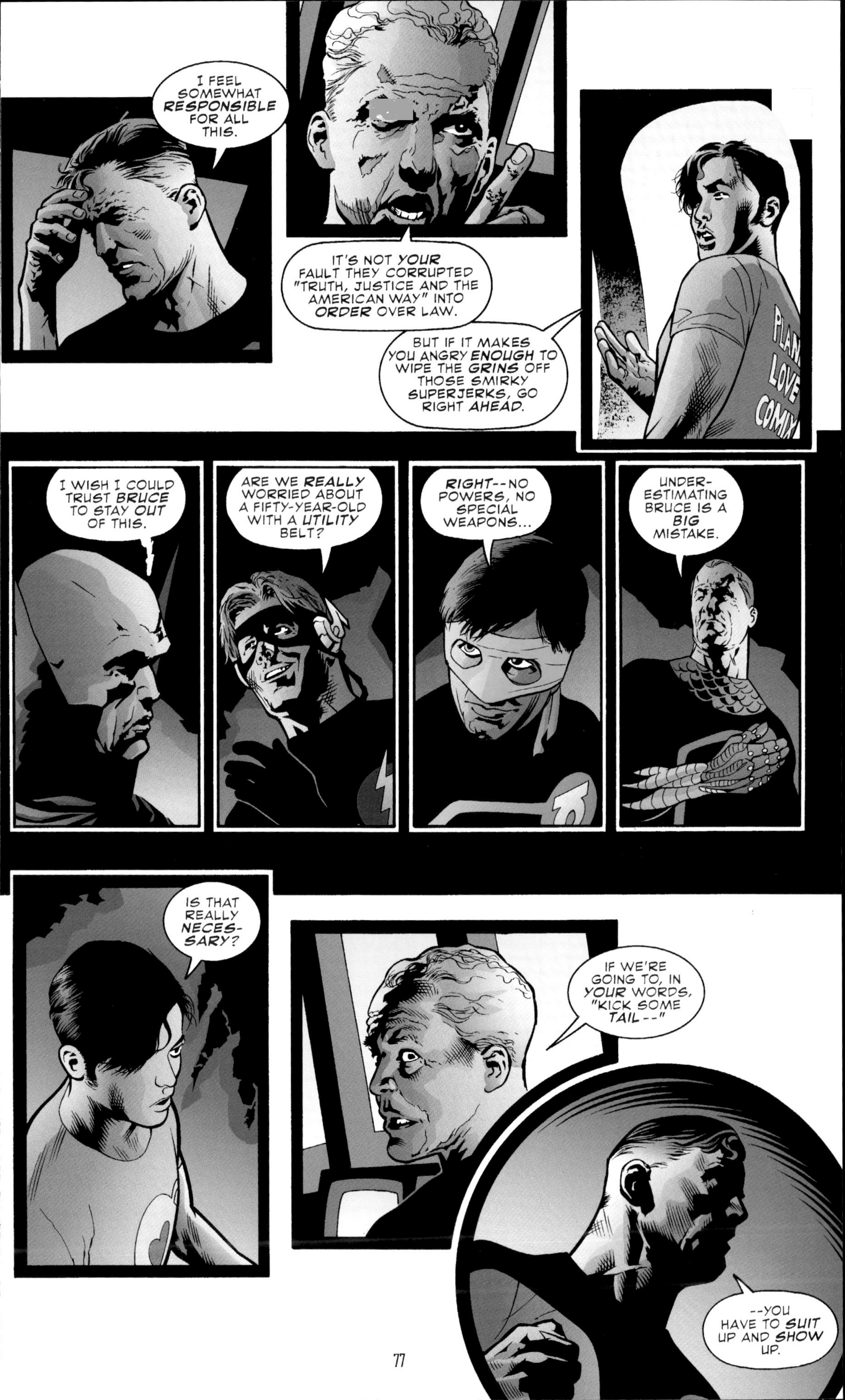
I FEEL SOMEWHAT RESPONSIBLE FOR ALL THIS.
IT'S NOT YOUR FAULT THEY CORRUPTED "TRUTH, JUSTICE AND THE AMERICAN WAY" INTO ORDER OVER LAW.
BUT IF IT MAKES YOU ANGRY ENOUGH TO WIPE THE GRINS OFF THOSE SMIRKY SUPERJERKS, GO RIGHT AHEAD.
I WISH I COULD TRUST BRUCE TO STAY OUT OF THIS.
ARE WE REALLY WORRIED ABOUT A FIFTY-YEAR-OLD WITH A UTILITY BELT?
RIGHT--NO POWERS, NO SPECIAL WEAPONS...
UNDER-ESTIMATING BRUCE IS A BIG MISTAKE.
IS THAT REALLY NECES-SARY?
IF WE'RE GOING TO, IN YOUR WORDS, "KICK SOME TAIL--"
--YOU HAVE TO SUIT UP AND SHOW UP.

TONIGHT'S *TOP STORY*--

SUPERMEN TERRORIST LEADER *PETER ROSS* AND HIS WIFE, *LANA LANG-ROSS*, SURRENDERED TO AUTHORITIES IN *LOS ANGELES* TODAY.

THE ACTION CAME AS A COMPLETE *SURPRISE* TO LAW ENFORCEMENT OFFICIALS, WHO HAD BEEN SEARCHING FOR THE TERRORIST SQUAD FOR OVER *THREE* YEARS.

IN *NATIONAL* NEWS--

--ALL SEVEN *MEMBERS* OF THE JUSTICE LEAGUE TODAY TENDERED THEIR *RESIGNATIONS*, EFFECTIVE *IMMEDIATELY*.

THIS ANNOUNCEMENT COMES JUST TWO *WEEKS* AFTER SUPERMAN'S VERY PUBLIC *RETURN*--

PAMELA ACKROYD

PAMELA ACKROYD

IN A JOINT *STATEMENT*, THE HEROES SAID THEY'RE QUITTING TO, AND I *QUOTE*, "SPEND MORE TIME WITH THEIR *FAMILIES*."

PRESIDENT DOLE WILL ANNOUNCE *REPLACEMENTS* BY THE END OF BUSINESS *FRIDAY*.

AND, SPEAKING OF *BUSINESS*--

IN A *RELATED* STORY, LEX LUTHOR HAS STEPPED DOWN AS CEO OF *LEXCORP*--

--AMID *RUMORS* OF A *FEDERAL* INVESTIGATION FOR TAX *FRAUD*.

IN *REACTION* TO THE SHAKEUP, LEXCORP STOCKS *PLUMMETED* SOME THIRTY DOLLARS A *SHARE*--

--BRINGING THE STOCK TO A *DECADE* LOW OF 75 AND 3/8 PER SHARE.

IN *OTHER* NEWS--

PAMELA ACKROYD

PAMELA ACKROYD

PAMELA ACKROYD

--BILLIONAIRE *BRUCE WAYNE* ANNOUNCED HE WILL SEEK THE DEMOCRATIC PARTY'S *NOMINATION* FOR PRESIDENT IN NEXT YEAR'S ELECTION.

WAYNE, WHO HAS *NEVER* HELD PUBLIC OFFICE, WAS A MAJOR *SUPPORTER* OF PRESIDENT DOLE IN *HER* PRESIDENTIAL RUN FOUR YEARS AGO.

I INTEND TO RUN ON A BROAD *PLATFORM* OF SOCIAL *REFORM*--

--TO *RETURN* TO THE PEOPLE OF THIS COUNTRY THE ECONOMIC *RIGHTS* THEY SO RICHLY *DESERVE*.

WE'LL BE *BACK*, RIGHT AFTER *THIS*...

PAMELA ACKROYD

PAMELA ACKROYD

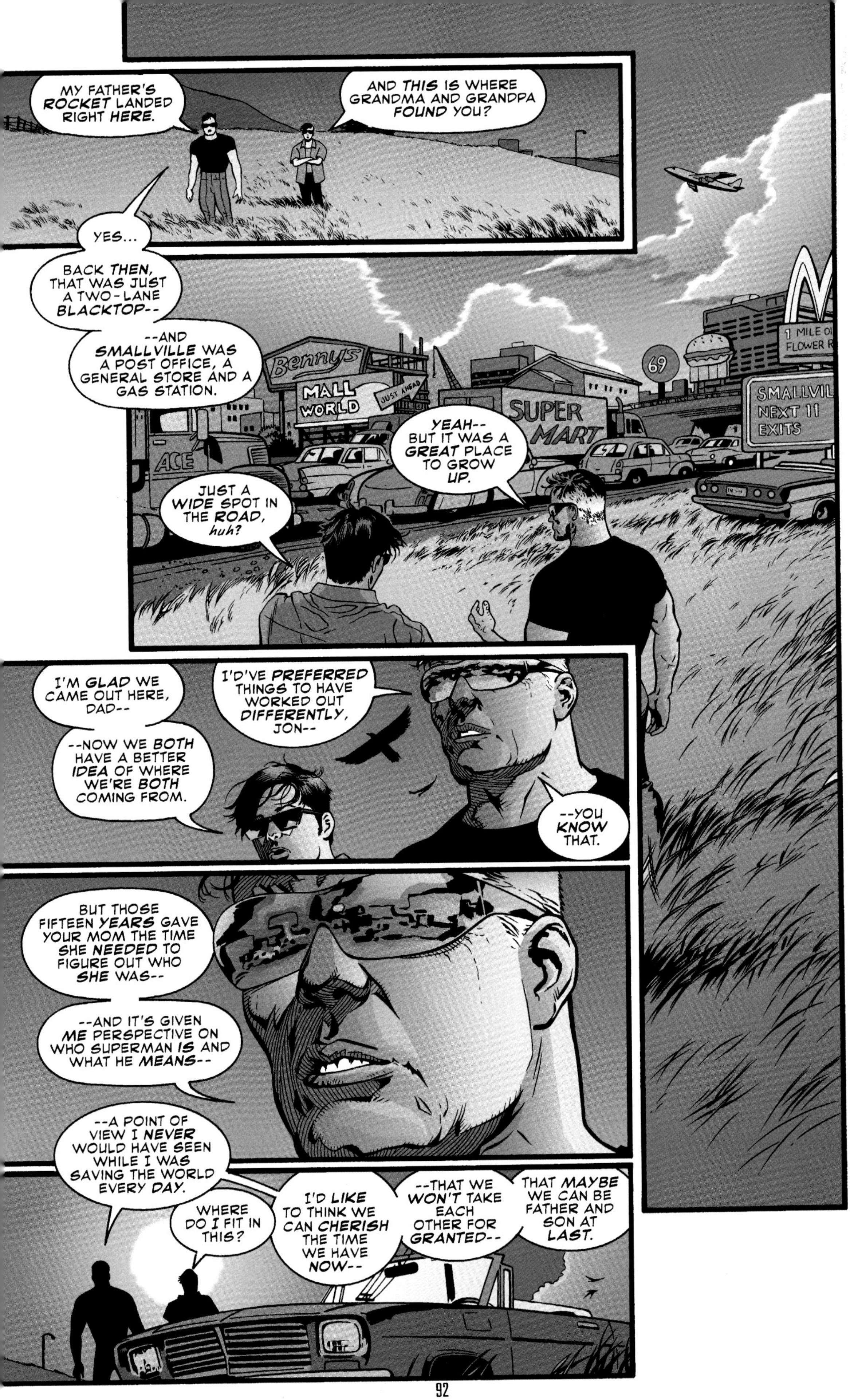
MY FATHER'S ROCKET LANDED RIGHT HERE.
AND THIS IS WHERE GRANDMA AND GRANDPA FOUND YOU?
YES...
BACK THEN, THAT WAS JUST A TWO-LANE BLACKTOP--
--AND SMALLVILLE WAS A POST OFFICE, A GENERAL STORE AND A GAS STATION.
Bennys
MALL WORLD
JUST AHEAD
SUPER MART
ACE
69
1 MILE O
FLOWER R
SMALLVIL
NEXT 11
EXITS
JUST A WIDE SPOT IN THE ROAD, huh?
YEAH-- BUT IT WAS A GREAT PLACE TO GROW UP.
I'M GLAD WE CAME OUT HERE, DAD--
--NOW WE BOTH HAVE A BETTER IDEA OF WHERE WE'RE BOTH COMING FROM.
I'D'VE PREFERRED THINGS TO HAVE WORKED OUT DIFFERENTLY, JON--
--YOU KNOW THAT.
BUT THOSE FIFTEEN YEARS GAVE YOUR MOM THE TIME SHE NEEDED TO FIGURE OUT WHO SHE WAS--
--AND IT'S GIVEN ME PERSPECTIVE ON WHO SUPERMAN IS AND WHAT HE MEANS--
--A POINT OF VIEW I NEVER WOULD HAVE SEEN WHILE I WAS SAVING THE WORLD EVERY DAY.
WHERE DO I FIT IN THIS?
I'D LIKE TO THINK WE CAN CHERISH THE TIME WE HAVE NOW--
--THAT WE WON'T TAKE EACH OTHER FOR GRANTED--
THAT MAYBE WE CAN BE FATHER AND SON AT LAST.

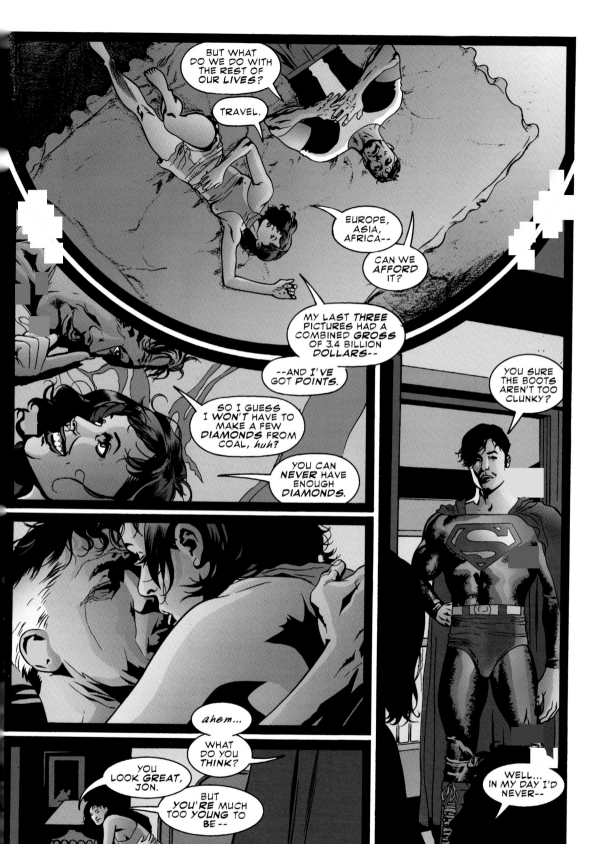

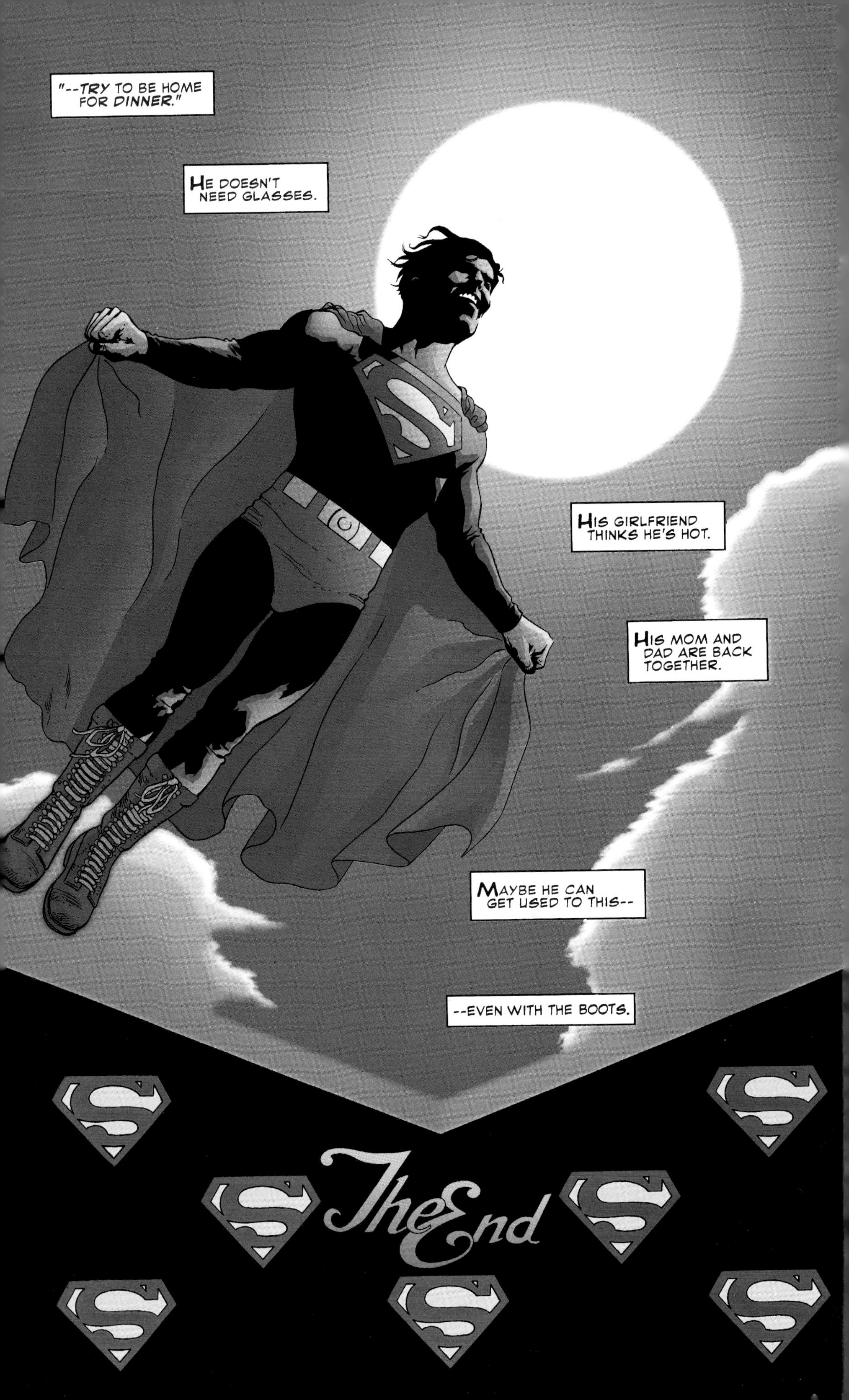
"--TRY TO BE HOME FOR DINNER."
HE DOESN'T NEED GLASSES.
HIS GIRLFRIEND THINKS HE'S HOT.
HIS MOM AND DAD ARE BACK TOGETHER.
MAYBE HE CAN GET USED TO THIS--
--EVEN WITH THE BOOTS.
The End